Butsko snarled and jumped to his feet. One of the Marine sergeants was on his knees, and Butsko kicked him in the teeth, then darted in the direction of the other Marine, who was on his feet, raising his arms to protect himself. Butsko punched toward his face, but the Marine's fists were raised to protect himself and he blocked the blow, although its force shook him up. The Marine swung down with a hook to Butsko's kidney and landed on target, but Butsko was too angry to feel pain. He grabbed the Marine by the throat and squeezed hard, and the Marine clawed at Butsko's hands, drawing blood, but Butsko wouldn't let go.

"Stop it!" Dolly screamed. "You'll kill him!"

Butsko heard her and came back to his senses. He loosened his grip and let the Marine, whose face now was blue, drop to the floor.

A crowd of women and servicemen were in the hallway, and one of the women screamed: "You killed him..."

Too Mean to Die

by
John Mackie

A JOVE BOOK

Excepting basic historical events, places, and personages, this series of books is fictional, and anything that appears otherwise is coincidental and unintentional.

The principal characters are imaginary, although they might remind veterans of specific men whom they knew. The Twenty-third Infantry Regiment, in which the characters serve, is used fictitiously—it doesn't represent the real historical Twenty-third Infantry, which has distinguished itself in so many battles from the Civil War to Vietnam—but it could have been any American line regiment that fought and bled during World War II.

These novels are dedicated to the men who were there. May their deeds and gallantry never be forgotten.

TOO MEAN TO DIE

A Jove book/published by arrangement with
the author

PRINTING HISTORY
Jove edition/July 1984

ISBN: 0-515-07648-1

Jove books are published by The Berkley Publishing Group,
200 Madison Avenue, New York, N.Y. 10016. The words
"A JOVE BOOK" and the "J" with sunburst are trademarks
belonging to Jove Publications, Inc.

PRINTED IN THE UNITED STATES OF AMERICA

Too Mean to Die

ONE . . .

The C-47 cargo plane made a wide right turn through the blue sky and came in low and steady for the landing. Master Sergeant John Butsko sat beside a window and looked at the hangars and administration buildings of Hickam Field whizzing past his eyes. His seat belt was tight and he wore a tan Class A uniform with his stripes on his sleeves and the blue Combat Infantryman's Badge above his left breast pocket. A smile creased his gnarled, battle-scarred face as he looked off into the distance toward the city of Honolulu, full of bars, whorehouses, and gambling dens. "Wow!" said Frankie La Barbara, sitting beside Butsko and rubbing the palms of his hands together. "We're here! Holy fuck, I don't believe it!"

The plane touched down, bounced, and touched down again. The wings flapped up and down and Frankie was afraid that one of them might drop off. He hadn't flown many times in his life and couldn't understand how something as big and heavy as a C-47 could sail through the air. The plane steadied itself and sped down the runway. Frankie chewed the wad of gum in his mouth, worked his shoulders, and sniffed the air nervously. This was his first furlough since he hit the Guadalcanal beach eight months earlier, and he couldn't wait to get into Honolulu.

Next to Frankie was Corporal Charles Bannon from Pecos, Texas, who was tall and rangy, tanned and weatherbeaten, with his cunt cap low on his forehead and tilted to the side. The first thing he wanted to do was get laid.

On the other side of Bannon was Pfc. Sam Longtree, a full-blooded Apache Indian from a reservation in Arizona. Longtree was quiet and expressionless, for he had been trained since youth not to show emotion, but he was anxious to get away from everything military and feel normal again.

The four of them were members of the reconnaisance platoon of the Twenty-third Infantry Regiment. The commander of the Twenty-third Infantry, Colonel William Stockton, had awarded them a seven-day furlough for the good work they'd done during a dangerous mission on the Jap-held island of New Georgia. The other survivors of the mission were in the hospital on Guadalcanal, recuperating from wounds.

The pilot turned down the flaps and hit the brakes. The big C-47 slowed and headed for the hangars. All the passengers sat on benches that lined both sides of the fuselage. Every seat was taken and gear was piled in the middle of the deck. Many of the passengers were officers, and the men from the recon platoon were on their best behavior, because they didn't want any trouble before they got into Honolulu.

The plane taxied to a stop and everyone fastened his seat belt. The officers stood up, and one of them took a pipe out of his shirt pocket, placing it in his mouth. He wore thick glasses and the insignia of the Medical Corps on his collar.

Butsko looked out the window and saw a staircase on wheels being rolled to the side of the plane by the ground crew. One of them climbed the stairs and fastened the staircase to the side of the plane. The door to the cockpit opened and one of the flyboys came out, a battered cap on his head and a grin on his face.

"Here we are," he said. "Welcome to Hawaii."

He opened the cargo door and all the soldiers stood up, gathering their gear together. The men from the recon platoon had nothing with them; they were lucky to have Class A uniforms that fit. Each of them carried over a hundred dollars in back pay in their pockets, and they'd buy whatever they needed.

They stood around impatiently, looking at each other, bending occasionally to peer out the window and see what was going on.

Some wounded soldiers were unloaded first, and then the officers filed up and marched out of the door, descending the staircase. After the last officer was out of the door there was a moment of hesitation, and then the GIs rushed toward the door, elbowing each other, pushing and cursing, causing a bottleneck.

"At ease!" Butsko shouted, watching them fighting to get out the door. He grabbed Frankie La Barbara by his wavy black hair and yanked him backward. "Line up and calm the fuck down!" He clutched another GI by the neck and slammed him against the fuselage of the plane.

The GIs heard Butsko's roaring voice and were scared shitless. They lined up as he said and filed out the door, climbing down the stairs. At the bottom were two MPs wearing chrome helmets and white gloves, checking papers.

"Have your orders ready," one of the MPs kept repeating over and over, as he looked at transfer orders, furlough authorizations, et cetera.

Bannon was the first man from the recon platoon out of the plane, and he looked up at the clear blue sky, the buildings scattered around the runway, and the B-17 bombers lined up on the apron. He felt weird, as if he were having a dream. Many times on Guadalcanal he thought he'd never see civilization again, and now here it was stretched out in front of him, peaceful and inviting. No bombs ever fell on Hawaii and it received no artillery bombardments. No Japanese soldiers would try to slit your throat while you were asleep at night.

In a daze Bannon walked down the ladder. He was so moved he thought he might cry. For seven days he'd be able to sleep in a real bed and walk down the streets of a real city. He'd be free from military discipline and could do whatever he liked.

"Have your papers ready," said the MP.

Bannon handed him the sheet of mimeographed orders signed by Colonel Stockton. The MP looked them over, glanced at the Combat Infantryman's Badge on Bannon's shirt, and handed him the orders back.

"Have a good time," said the MP, "but stay out of trouble."

"Yo," said Bannon.

3

Bannon stood to the side and waited for the others. Frankie La Barbara thrust his orders at the MP, snapped his gun, and shifted nervously from foot to foot. Like Bannon, he wore his cunt cap low over his eyes and slanted to the side. His khaki shirt was a little too small and looked as though it would burst its buttons if he breathed too hard. The MP handed the orders back to Frankie and he folded them into his shirt pocket, moving toward Bannon.

"Rear echelon assholes," Frankie muttered. "I been getting shot at since last summer and they treat me like a fucking convict."

"Keep your voice down."

"I'd like to see them start something with me. I'd just like to see them."

Bannon turned away from Frankie, because he didn't want to take any chances with the MPs. Longtree came through the line next, his face like stone, with superb military bearing. The MP checked his orders, and Longtree sauntered toward Bannon and Frankie La Barbara.

"Whataya think of them MPs?" Frankie asked Longtree, a little too loudly. "Ain't they something?"

"You talk too much, Frankie," Longtree said.

"Yeah, well, I ain't afraid of them fucking MPs," Frankie said. "If I ain't afraid of Japs, I sure as hell ain't afraid of MPs."

One of the MPs turned his head around. "You say something, soldier?"

"Who, me?" Frankie asked, pointing his thumb to his chest.

"Yeah, you."

"I didn't say nothing. You must be hearing things, buddy."

The MP turned around as Butsko held out his orders. Frankie snickered in the background, and the MP looked at him again.

"You better watch your step, soldier," the MP said ominously.

"Don't worry about me," Frankie replied. "Worry about yourself."

The MP reached for his stick and felt a firm hand on his wrist. It was Butsko with a big smile on his face.

"He's one of my men," Butsko said. "I'll take care of him."

The MP looked at the scars on Butsko's face, the master sergeant's stripes on his shoulders, the Combat Infantryman's

4

Badge on his shirt. Butsko had a big head with thick black hair, and his cunt cap was so small it looked as if it would topple off over his nose.

"Combat fatigue," Butsko said with a wink. "He can't help himself. I'll watch him."

"Sure thing, Sarge," the MP said.

Butsko folded his orders into his back pocket and walked toward the other three men from his recon platoon, glowering at Frankie La Barbara.

"Hey, what I do?" Frankie said.

"Shut up!" Butsko muttered.

Frankie wasn't afraid of many people in the world, but he was scared to death of Butsko.

"Frankie," Butsko said, "someday you're gonna wind up in a jackpot if you're not careful."

"I know what I'm doing, Sarge. Don't worry about me."

"I'm not worried about you, kid. I'm just telling you for your own good."

They walked across the airfield, and the hot afternoon sun beat down upon them. Soldiers, pilots, and mechanics strolled about near the hangars, while planes flew around in the sky. Bannon, Longtree, and Frankie La Barbara followed Butsko, who knew his way around because he'd been stationed nearby at Schofield Barracks for a few years before the war.

Butsko led them to an opening in the chain fence that bordered the airfield. Two MPs guarded the opening, and once again the GIs had to show their orders. The MPs waved them through and the GIs found themselves on a sidewalk next to a curb where military vehicles were parked bumper to bumper. Jeeps, three-quarter-ton trucks, and Chevrolets painted khaki drove by on the street. It reminded Bannon of when he was in basic training at Fort Ord, California. He was assailed by confusing thoughts. On one hand he wished he could be stationed here, far from the grim and bloody war, and on the other hand he felt contempt for the men he saw, because he didn't consider them real soldiers.

Butsko walked confidently down the sidewalk, his big shoulders squared and his eyes straight ahead. The other three gawked at everything like visitors from another planet, which in a sense they were. Hickam Field on Hawaii was a radically different world for them from Guadalcanal.

5

They heard an explosion and all of them, including Butsko, hit the dirt instinctively. It was only a truck backfiring on the street near them, and they got up sheepishly, brushing off their uniforms. Soldiers nearby looked at them curiously, and they continued down the street.

Frankie La Barbara spotted two WACs on the other side of the street and took off like a bolt of lightning, while the others kept following Butsko. Frankie held his hat on his head and dodged trucks and jeeps in the middle of the street, defying death itself to get closer to the women. They saw him coming and pretended not to notice. One was a blonde and the other a brunette; they were nothing special.

But to Frankie La Barbara, after all those months on Guadalcanal, every woman was special. He jumped onto the sidewalk in front of them and winked, chewing his gum ferociously.

"Howya doing, girls?" he said with a big smile.

They glanced at him and passed him by as if he were a green light. They had their reputations to maintain, and it wouldn't do to let themselves be picked up by an ordinary GI in broad daylight on Hickam Field.

Frankie ran after them and got in front of them again, walking backward, grinning and gesticulating with his hands. "Hey, what's the hurry? Is there a law around here against talking to soldiers?" He pointed to the blonde. "Don't I know you from someplace? Where you from, sweetheart?"

Nothing worked. The WACs kept walking, ignoring him. Frankie was the persistent type and would have hounded them forever, but he noticed Butsko and the others moving farther away and realized he'd probably have better luck in Honolulu.

"See you later, girls," Frankie said, taking off his cap. "I gotta go, and when you gotta go, you gotta go. Watch out for all the VD that's going around."

The girls raised their eyebrows, and Frankie dashed off into the street again, threaded his way through the traffic, and made it to the other side, where he ran to catch up with Butsko and the others.

"Coupla fucking skags," Frankie muttered, catching up with them. "Not worth the trouble."

They came to a bus stop, where several soldiers were waiting on benches, leaning against the telephone poles, or standing

6

with their hands in their pockets underneath the roof shelter that would protect them if it rained.

"The bus into town stops here," Butsko said, reaching into his shirt pocket for his package of Luckies. He took one out and lit it with his old Zippo.

All the men lit up cigarettes and looked in the direction from which the bus would come. They were eager to get into town and cut loose. The faint breeze rustled the leaves of the palms trees nearby. A lieutenant approached and all the soldiers at the bus stop snapped to attention and threw highballs. The lieutenant saluted back and walked by, and the men from Guadalcanal noticed that he wasn't wearing the Combat Infantryman's Badge, which meant that he was a rear-echelon soldier and not really worth their respect.

Frankie spat into the gutter. "Cocksucker probably pushes papers around all day, and he thinks he a soldier."

"Hey, Frankie," Bannon said, "you never got anything good to say about anybody."

"Fuck off, cowboy."

Butsko's ears perked up, because he heard soldiers counting cadence not far away. He turned around and saw road guards moving toward the intersection, standing at parade rest and stopping traffic. They wore fatigues, helmets, and cartridge belts, and carried M 1 rifles. A few moments later the main body of soldiers came marching through the intersection. At their side was a grizzled old sergeant wearing his helmet so low over his eyes it was a miracle that he could see anything.

"Sound off!" sang the old sergeant.

"One-two!" replied the soldiers.

"Sound off!"

"Three-four!"

"Cadence count!"

"One-two-three-four-one-two . . . three-four!"

The sergeant kicked a soldier in the ass because he was out of step, and straightened the rifle of another soldier. He returned to his position at the side of the formation and resumed the cadence.

"I don't know but I been told . . . !"

"I don't know but I been told . . . !"

". . . Eskimo Pussy is mighty cold!"

7

"... Eskimo pussy is mighty cold!"

"Sound off!"

Butsko couldn't suppress a grin. They were still marching to the same old silly shit. He used to march men around the same way in the old peacetime Army, but that seemed long ago and far away to him. The group of men passed through the intersection, counting cadence, and then the road guards pulled back to the formation, permitting the traffic to resume. Butsko still could hear them sounding off.

"AWOL, AWOL, where you been?"

"AWOL, AWOL, where you been?"

"Down in Honolulu, drinking gin!"

"Down in Honolulu drinking gin!"

"Sound off!"

Butsko puffed his cigarette and turned around.

"Here comes the bus," Bannon said.

Butsko looked at it, painted OD green like everything else in sight. The other soldiers were lining up, and Butsko took another drag from his cigarette as his men joined the rear of the line. Butsko got behind them and thought about Dolly, his wife, who lived in Honolulu. He hadn't heard from her in a long time and he hadn't written her, either, although they were legally married and she was receiving his allotment. They'd broken up in the summer of 1941 after he'd punched her in the mouth a few times. He'd found out that she was carrying on with other guys, so he got a little drunk and worked her over. After a few months in the Schofield Barracks post stockade, they'd shipped him to the Phillipines just in time for the Japanese invasion. Butsko had been on the Bataan Death March, escaped from a Jap POW camp in northern Luzon, and survived to fight another day.

The soldiers loaded onto the bus. Butsko was the last one on. Bannon sat beside Longtree. Frankie was sitting all by himself, but Butsko didn't feel like sitting next to Frankie all the way into Honolulu, listening to his bullshit, so Butsko sat alone on the wide bench at the rear of the bus.

The driver shifted into gear and headed toward the main gate. Butsko looked out the window at two-story wooden barracks and wondered if he ought to visit Dolly while he was in Honolulu or just get drunk and go to a whorehouse.

Somehow he couldn't make up his mind. He wanted to see

8

Dolly, because he still felt something for her, but he also didn't want to see her, because she had the capacity to piss him off, and he didn't want to wind up in the stockade again. The Schofield Barracks post stockade was notorious for its brutality and oppressive living conditions. It had been almost as bad as that Jap POW camp on Luzon.

I'll have a few drinks as soon as I hit Honolulu. Butsko thought. *Then I'll make up my mind.*

TWO . . .

Colonel William Stockton, commanding officer of the Twenty-third Infantry Regiment, sat behind his desk in a new quonset hut on Guadalcanal and looked over rosters of men and officers being assigned to his regiment.

The Twenty-third was gradually being brought to full strength for the campaign that everyone knew would begin soon on New Georgia, the next island up the Solomon chain from Guadalcanal. General MacArthur and Admiral Nimitz wanted the Jap airfields on New Georgia so they could bomb enemy strongholds on Bougainville and New Britain, which were the key islands in that part of the South Pacific. With the Solomon Islands in US possession, and New Guinea under control, MacArthur would then be free to invade the Philippines, and Nimitz could rip into the Gilbert and Mariana Islands, heading directly toward Japan itself.

Colonel Stockton had not yet been told of the role the Twenty-third Regiment would play in the invasion of New Georgia, but he hoped it would be significant. He'd already presented his own invasion strategy to General Hawkins, the commander of the Eighty-first Division, but hadn't heard anything about it yet. Colonel Stockton was a professional soldier and he wanted his regiment to spearhead the invasion. He was always afraid of being shunted aside where he wouldn't be noticed and where his career would languish.

There was a knock on his door.

"Yes?" he said.

The door opened and Sergeant Major Ramsay entered his office. Ramsay closed the door behind him and walked to Colonel Stockton's desk, bending over it and saying softly: "There's a General Oglesby out there who says he wants to speak with you, sir."

Colonel Stockton smiled, because General Oglesby was an old friend of his. "Send him in," Colonel Stockton said.

"Yes, sir."

Ramsay turned around and left Colonel Stockton's office, while Colonel Stockton smoothed down his silvery hair and made sure there were no tobacco ashes on his shirt. The door opened again and General Oglesby entered, a tall gangly man with a big nose, who reminded Stockton of a bird of prey.

Colonel Stockton stood at attention and saluted, and General Oglesby saluted back.

"How are you, Bill?" General Oglesby said, holding out his hand.

Colonel Stockton shook it. "Not bad—how about you?"

"Can't complain."

"When did you arrive on Guadalcanal?"

"This morning," General Oglesby replied, sitting on a chair in front of Colonel Stockton's desk.

Colonel Stockton returned to his seat, and both men looked at each other for a few moments. They'd been in the same cadet company at West Point and graduated in the same class. Now Oglesby was a general on the staff of General MacArthur in Australia, and Stockton was still a colonel working out of a quonset hut in the jungle. They hadn't seen each other for about two years.

"What brings you to Guadalcanal?" Colonel Stockton asked.

"The New Georgia invasion."

"Are the plans set?"

"Yep."

"What part will we be playing."

"As it stands right now, the Eighty-first Division will be in reserve."

Colonel Stockton closed his eyes. "Shit."

"Don't let it get you down. I'm sure you'll see action before the campaign is over."

"Who's going in first?"

"Right now we're planning three landings. A lot of units will take part, but the bulk of the men will be from the Forty-third Division."

"But they're all green!"

"They have to learn somewhere."

"They're the ones who should be in reserve, Frank. If those green soldiers meet heavy resistance, they won't get far."

"They're going ashore in most places with seasoned units, including Marines, and if the offensive stalls, then we'll move in our tough guys, like the ones in your regiment." General Oglesby smiled.

"Hell," said Colonel Stockton, "we're pretty green ourselves." He held up the rosters of new men. "Only about thirty-five percent of my original regiment is fit for duty."

"You've done a great job here on Guadalcanal, Bill."

Colonel Stockton shrugged bitterly. "It hasn't done me much good."

"Oh, yes it has."

"You know something I don't, Frank?"

General Oglesby leaned back in his chair. "You're up for a star, Bill."

"I am?"

"Yep."

Colonel Stockton closed his eyes. More than anything in the world, he wanted the star of a brigadier general on his collar. "What are my chances?"

"It's all up to the old man."

"General MacArthur?"

General Oglesby nodded.

Colonel Stockton took his old briar out of his ashtray and filled it with Briggs smoking mixture. He'd never met General MacArthur, although he'd seen him many times at military functions. He thought MacArthur was a talented strategist and field commander, but in recent years he'd become sort of a ham actor. "How much do you think MacArthur knows about me?"

"Everything important." Colonel Oglesby looked away for a few moments. "There's only one thing that could go against you."

"My wife?"

"Right."

"But the son of a bitch is divorced himself!"

"That's true, but his wife didn't run off with a captain in the Air Corps."

Stockton flinched as if he'd been slapped in the face.

"Sorry about that, Bill," General Oglesby said, "but if there's going to be a problem, that's the direction it'll come from. I'm giving you the straight poop. I'm not going to hem and haw with you."

"I appreciate that, Frank."

The room fell silent as Colonel Stockton lit his pipe. General Oglesby took out a cigarette. Colonel Stockton knew that the Army didn't fool around when it gave out generals' stars. You had to be an outstanding officer, and your personal life had to be in reasonable order. A man whose wife drank too much and made a fool of him by running off with a young captain in the Air Corps, didn't have his personal life in reasonable order.

Colonel Stockton puffed his pipe, and his head disappeared in a cloud of blue smoke. "That bitch!" he said viciously.

General Oglesby smiled. "Well, you've never had very good taste in women, Bill. All your women have been pretty—don't get me wrong—but they've all been a little on the strange side."

"Most pretty women are on the strange side," Colonel Stockton muttered.

"Maybe you should have married one who wasn't so pretty, but who would've been a good wife."

"It's too late for that now." Colonel Stockton wrinkled his brow. "But hell, Frank, there's a war on. I think the ability to command troops in battle should take a certain precedence, and I think my Twenty-third Regiment has done pretty damn well. We've kicked the shit out of the Japs ever since we landed on this goddamn island, except for a few setbacks here and there, and hell, we were the ones who cracked the Gifu Line,

14

which was the toughest Jap stronghold on Guadalcanal. Doesn't that mean anything?"

"It means a lot," General Oglesby said. "I'd say if it weren't for your wife, you might have the star in the bag, but to be honest with you, you're not the only colonel in the Army with an excellent combat record, and there aren't that many stars around."

"I get it," Colonel Stockton said. "The competition is tough."

"Very tough."

"Well, since I can't do anything about Jennifer, I guess I'll just have to do better on the job."

"That's one way to look at it. Of course, you can rely on me to put in a good word for you every now and then with the old man."

"I appreciate that, Frank."

"We go back a long way together, Bill. I'll do everything for you that I can."

THREE . . .

The bus stopped in front of the terminal and the soldiers unloaded onto the sidewalk. The men from the recon platoon had
sat toward the rear of the bus and now moved forward eagerly,
bending down to look out the windows as men hopped down
from the bus one by one. They saw other servicemen and seedy
buildings that housed bars, pawnshops, penny arcades, and
businesses that sold insignia and other uniform items to servicemen.

"Where's the fucking broads?" Frankie asked. "Ain't there
no broads in this fucking city?"

Frankie was the first one off the bus, and the first thing he
did was reach for his package of cigarettes. He looked all
around him and his hands trembled because he didn't know
what to do first. Bannon got off the bus next.

"Looks like every bus terminal in every town I ever been
in," he said. "The only thing different about this place is the
palm trees."

"I need a drink," Frankie said, "and then I'm gonna get
laid."

Longtree stepped down from the bus and glanced around

17

stiffly, still not showing any emotion, although he wanted to do a war whoop.

"Where you headed, Chief?" Frankie asked.

"Don't know yet."

Butsko joined them, taking out his pack of Luckies. "Well, here we are," he said, spearing one between his thick lips. "I'll see you guys later. Stay out of trouble."

"Hey, Sarge," Bannon said, "where's a good cathouse around here."

"There ain't no good cathouses around here," Butsko replied. "You have to go down to the docks if you want to go to a good cathouse."

"Which way's the docks?"

Before Butsko could answer, Frankie La Barbara cut in: "Is there a good gambling joint around here?"

"Not in this part of town."

Longtree took his turn. "Is there some quiet place where a man can be alone?"

Butsko looked at the faces of his three men and realized they needed him. He had to tell them what to do and where to go, otherwise they'd get all fucked up in Honolulu and piss their money away.

"Let's go into one of these gin mills and have a drink," Butsko said. "I'll tell you what you need to know."

He led them underneath the three bronze balls of a pawnshop into a saloon called The First Base Cafe. It was full of soldiers, sailors, and Marines getting drunk out of their minds, waiting for buses or just getting off them and needing to moisten their mouths. A jukebox was playing Benny Goodman, and middle-aged waitresses with an excess of makeup on their faces carried beer bottles and shot glasses to customers sitting in the booths. They were the only women in the joint.

The men from the recon platoon elbowed their way up to the bar, and Butsko sidled between two sailors sitting on stools, raising his hand in the air.

"Hey, barkeep!" he said.

"Be with you in a moment!" replied the bartender, pouring cheap whiskey into a row of shot glasses while the other bartender clanged the cash register.

"Wow," said Frankie La Barbara. "These fucking people

18

are making money hand over fist. Would I like to have a piece of this place."

"What're you drinking?" Butsko asked him.

"Anything—I don't give a fuck."

"How about you?" Butsko asked Bannon.

"Whatever you're having," Bannon said.

"Me too," Longtree added.

Butsko leaned over the bar. "Hey, barkeep!" he shouted.

"I said I'll be right with you!"

Butsko frowned and turned around, brushing against the sailor to his left.

"Hey, who the fuck you pushing!" said the sailor.

"Shaddup before I put your face through the bar," Butsko replied.

The sailor took a closer look at Butsko's face and saw the scars and sheer brutality written all over it. He also noticed Butsko's Combat Infantryman's Badge. The sailor decided to shut up and drink his beer.

Butsko looked at Bannon. "The best cathouse in town—at least in the old days, anyway—is the Curtis Hotel on Seaview Avenue, near the docks. Write it down."

"I can remember it."

Frankie appeared interested. "Good-looking babes there?"

"I thought you wanted to gamble."

"Maybe I'll do a little fucking first."

"If you wanna gamble, they have good games in back of the Pineapple Pool Room, also down near the docks. I don't remember the street, but you can probably find it in a phone book."

"Got it," Frankie said.

The bartender appeared behind Butsko. "What'll you have, buddy."

Butsko turned around and looked at the bartender, a big overweight man who had a lot of muscle under his fat. "Four double whiskies straight up," he said.

The bartender poured the drinks, and Butsko looked. "If you wanna be alone, Chief, get yourself a good hotel room—that's all I can tell you. But I don't know how alone that's gonna be, because I imagine every hotel in town is full to the rafters with servicemen walking around drunk, screaming and hollering; you know what servicemen are like once they get a few drinks in them." Butsko turned around and motioned with his hands. "Like this."

Men laughed, shouted, and cursed all around them. One of them pinched the fat bottom of a waitress and she hit him over the head with her round little tray, causing more laughing and whooping.

Butsko glanced about disapprovingly. "What a fucking bust-out joint this place turned out to be."

"Two dollars," said the bartender.

Butsko turned around and threw two one-dollar bills and some change on the bar. Then he picked up the double shot glasses and passed them around. He raised his shot glass into the air. "To the gang back on Guadalcanal," Butsko said.

The men clicked glasses and gulped down some whiskey. Frankie wrinkled his nose and turned down the corners of his lips. "Jesus, who pissed in my glass?" he said.

"I've drunk worse," Bannon replied.

"You're a fucking cowboy, what do you know?"

Longtree savored the sweet burning sensation of the whiskey as it trickled down his throat. It made him feel warm and his mind became light. He hadn't drunk any whiskey for a long time.

Butsko drained his glass in two gulps and didn't bat an eye. He wiped his mouth with the back of his hand. "Hey, barkeep—four refills here!"

"Coming up," said the bartender.

Bannon reached into his pocket. "I'll get this round," he said.

"Keep your fucking money where it is," Butsko replied. "I got it."

"You got the last one."

"I said keep your fucking money where it is. You guys don't make shit."

The sailor next to Butsko was feeling uncomfortable with all the big soldiers crowding around him, and he decided to drink someplace else. He stood unsteadily, pushed away from the bar, and headed for the door, angling a little to one side and then to another, as if on the deck of a ship in high seas.

Bannon pointed to the barstool. "Have a seat, Sarge."

"I'm okay. Sit down yourself, kid."

"I'm not tired."

"Well, I am," said Frankie La Barbara, sitting on the stool. "Hey, bartender!" he shouted. "You make this whiskey out of old combat boots?"

The bartender frowned as he pushed forward four more double shots. Butsko threw his money on the bar and passed out the glasses.

"Who'll we drink to this time?" asked Frankie La Barbara.

"Who'd we drink to last time?" asked Butsko.

"The guys back on Guadalcanal," replied Longtree.

"Well, this time let's drink to Colonel Stockton, because without that old gray-haired tight-assed son of a bitch, we wouldn't be here." Butsko raised his glass in the air. "To Colonel Stockton!"

"To Colonel Stockton!" the other three repeated.

They all slugged their whiskey down. The record on the jukebox changed and Carmen Miranda came on, singing about bananas.

"She can sit on my banana any day," said Frankie La Barbara.

"Who?" asked Butsko.

"That girl in the jukebox."

"Oh," said Butsko. He hadn't been paying any attention to the jukebox. He was still thinking about Colonel Stockton. "You know, the colonel ain't a bad guy," he said. "He's one of the best officers I ever served under. Really knows his stuff. Let's have another drink to the colonel."

"My glass is empty," said Longtree, who felt himself becoming a little woozy already.

"I'll order another round." Butsko waved to the bartender. "Hey, Charlie, let's have another round over here!"

"My name ain't Charlie!" replied the bartender.

"Just gimme another round over here!"

"Wait your turn!"

"Wait my turn," Butsko grumbled, turning around. "This fucking gin mill is a real shithouse."

"You brought us here," said Frankie.

"It was the closest place."

Bannon looked at the bottles stacked on the back of the bar. "Reminds me of a place back home," he said, "only we had a band."

"What'd they play?" Frankie asked. "Shitkicker music?"

"Fuck you."

Butsko slapped Longtree on the arm. "How you doing, Chief?"

"Okay, Sarge."

"You know," Butsko said, wiping his mouth with the back of his hand, "you're a damn fine soldier, Chief."

"Thanks, Sarge."

"I mean it. I really do mean it."

"I know you do, Sarge."

"Don't know what we'd do without you."

"You'd just put some other asshole on the point."

"There's nobody like you, Chief, and I really mean it."

"Hey," Frankie said to Butsko, "what about me?"

"What about you?"

"You ain't never said nothing good to me, Sarge."

"That's because you're a fucking goldbrick, Frankie. Couple times I thought of shooting you, you know that?"

"Yeah?" asked Frankie, stunned.

"Yeah," replied Butsko.

The bartender set down the four glasses. "Two bucks," he said.

"While you're here, Charlie," Butsko told him, "you might as well pour us another round."

"My name isn't Charlie," the bartender said.

"Yeah? What is it?"

"Just call me *bartender*."

"Okay, Charlie."

The bartender frowned as he set more glasses on the bar. Butsko drained the glass he was drinking and then picked up a drink that the bartender had just served.

"To Colonel Stockton!" he said.

The others drank their double shots quickly and took fresh glasses. They clicked glasses, and Butsko, his face flushed and his eyes starting to glaze over, decided to make a speech.

"To the colonel!" he said. "To the only officer worth a fiddler's fuck in the entire Army! And to the Twenty-third Regiment, the toughest sons of bitches in the world!"

Frankie grunted. "You mean to the biggest bunch of assholes in the world!"

22

"What was that?" Butsko said.

"Nothing, Sarge."

Butsko took another gulp of whiskey, and it tasted fine. He looked around and everybody seemed to be floating through the air. Emotion overcame him and he burst into song.

"Two bucks!" interrupted the bartender.

"You again?" Butsko asked, reaching into his pocket.

"Yeah, me again," said the bartender.

Frankie beat out Butsko and threw his money on the bar. "Here you go, big-time," he said to the bartender.

Butsko tapped Frankie on the shoulder with the back of his hand. "You know, Frankie, you're not a bad guy at all."

"Yeah?" Frankie said. "I thought you didn't like me."

"I like you, Frankie," Butsko replied. "If I didn't like you, I wouldn't be here talking to you right now. You got your head up your ass most of the time, but you're a fighter. I always know I can depend on you when the shit hits the fan."

Frankie was pleased. This was the first time Butsko had ever said anything nice to him, and he didn't know what to say.

Butsko wiggled his glass in the air. "Here's looking at you," he said, and raised it to his lips.

The men drained their glasses and dropped them on the bar. By now they were all a little whacked out. Tommy Dorsey and his orchestra were playing on the jukebox, and the Marine in front of Butsko got up and went to the toilet. Butsko dropped onto the Marine's stool.

Bannon was looking at the bottles on the back of the bar. It reminded him of the night in Pecos, Texas, when he was sitting at a bar in a little dive and the most beautiful girl in the world walked in. He said something to her—he didn't remember exactly what right now—and she said something back, and that had been the beginning of the love affair that was still supposed to be going on, although he hadn't seen her in over a year, and on top of that, he had gotten married to a native girl on Guadalcanal a little while back. Bannon didn't know what to do about the native girl, because things had cooled considerably between them. She didn't speak much English and he didn't speak any of her language, so there wasn't a hell

23

of a lot to hold them together after the fucking was over.

Fresh double-shot glasses were on the bar, and Bannon grabbed one of them.

"Who we drinking to this time?" Bannon asked.

Butsko narrowed his eyes and a little drool seeped from the corner of his mouth. "You wanna know something, Bannon?"

"What?"

"You're the best fucking soldier in the platoon, except for me."

"I am?"

"Yeah." Butsko burped. "Just thought I'd tell you."

There was embarrassed silence for a few moments, and Butsko was more embarrassed than anybody else. He'd never spoken to his men like this, but they were all getting drunk and they were in a strange environment. Butsko put his hand on Bannon's shoulder and looked him in the eye.

"You're smart as a whip and you've got balls of steel," Butsko said to Bannon. "You saved my life on Tassafaronga Point, and don't think I forgot it."

Bannon didn't know what to say. Frankie snickered nervously because tender moments made him uncomfortable.

"You been drinking too much of that cheap whiskey," Frankie said. "Next thing you'll be taking us to the nearest church."

"You need to go to church," Butsko said, "because you're a bad egg, Frankie. You don't think straight. You think crooked. You're gonna get yourself in a real jam someday, and I won't be able to get you out of it."

"Don't worry about me, Sarge. I can take care of myself."

"Bullshit."

Butsko drained his glass and brought it down with a slam on the bar. "Hey, Charlie, set 'em up over here!"

A chubby waitress walked by and Butsko winked at her, but the waitress kept walking. An argument started up in a corner where a bunch of servicemen were playing bumper pool. The Marine came back from the shithouse and looked at Butsko.

"Hey," said the Marine, "you're sitting on my stool."

"I didn't see your name writ on it," Butsko replied.

"But I was sitting on it!"

"Well, I'm sitting on it now."

The Marine was a red-faced young man with big jug ears

and freckles on his nose. The Marine Corps had no equivalent of the Combat Infantryman's Badge, but he wore a strip of combat ribbons above his left shirt pocket. A few Marines who'd been standing nearby moved a little closer to the argument.

The Marine looked Butsko over and wondered how far to take it. Butsko was big and ugly, a master sergeant in the infantry, but the young Marine was no coward, and he wanted to uphold the honor of the Marine Corps.

"I think you'd better get up, Sergeant," the Marine said, moving his legs apart and planting his feet firmly on the floor.

Now the ball was in Butsko's court. He could lay the kid out with one punch and start a big brawl, or he could give the kid the bar stool and cool out the situation. Butsko had seven days of furlough coming to him, and he didn't want any problems. Fuck it, he'd give the kid the barstool.

Butsko stood up and grinned. "I guess you need it more than I do, kid." He slapped the stool with his hand. "Here you go."

Now the young Marine felt bad, because Butsko was older than he and had more rank. "Naw, that's all right," the Marine said with a wave of his hand. "Forget about it."

Butsko slapped the seat again. "C'mon sit down."

"I been sitting down too much anyways," the Marine replied. "I think I'll stretch my legs for a while."

"What're you drinking?" Butsko asked.

"Whiskey and ginger ale."

"Hey, Charlie!" Butsko shouted to the bartender. "Give this young Marine here a whiskey and ginger ale!"

"I told you that my name ain't Charlie!"

"Stop breaking my hump," Butsko told him, and then turned to the Marine. "What's your name, kiddo?"

"Harrison."

"I'm Butsko, and this is Bannon, La Barbara, and Longtree."

They shook hands all around, and some of the sailors and Marines standing in the vicinity got into the act, introducing themselves and shaking hands. Soon a substantial group of servicemen was huddling around Butsko and the others from the recon platoon.

"What outfit you with?" Butsko said to the Marine.

"The Seventh Marines."

"The Seventh Marines! Then you musta been on Guadalcanal?"

"Your fucking-A-well-John I was on Guadalcanal," said the young Marine.

"Well, we're from the Twenty-third Infantry."

"No shit!"

"No shit."

The Marine motioned with his hand. "These guys here with me are from the Seventh Marines too!"

"No shit!"

"No shit!"

"Well, I'll be good-go-to-hell!" Butsko exclaimed. "Charlie, a round of drinks for my friends here!"

"My name ain't Charlie!" the bartender said angrily.

Butsko leaned over the bar and looked him in the eye. "It is now," he said.

The young Marine leaned over the bar too. "That's right."

"You heard what the man said," Frankie La Barbara snarled at the bartender.

All the GIs and Marines looked menacingly at the bartender, and he backed down. He thought he might be able to handle one or two of them, but he knew he couldn't handle all of them. Actually, he couldn't even handle one of them, because they were all combat soldiers and he was just a big guy who thought he was tough.

"What'll you guys have?" the bartender asked, trying to smile.

The GIs and Marines told him what they wanted, and he picked bottles off the bar, mixing the drinks. A waitress threaded her way through the group of men and they whistled seductively, but she kept going as if she didn't hear anything. On the jukebox the Andrews Sisters came on and sang "Don't Sit Under the Apple Tree With Anybody Else But Me." Some of the men sang along, thinking of their wives and girl friends back home.

Butsko looked at his watch. It was four o'clock in the afternoon. He hadn't intended to spend so much time with the men in his platoon, but now he wondered why he'd been so eager to get away from them. After all, they were his men, his blood brothers practically, and he had become closer to them than

26

anybody else in the world. He felt closer to them than to his real family back in McKeesport, Pennsylvania, and even to his wife, Dolly, who was no good and had never been any good. Bannon even had saved his life once, and all the others had never let him down when the bullets were flying on Guadalcanal.

He was a little drunk, and some whiskey trickled out the corner of his mouth when he drank from his glass. "You know," he said with slur, "I love you fucking guys."

Frankie La Barbara guffawed. "Gimme a break, willya, Sarge?"

"I mean it," Butsko said, pushing his cunt cap to the back of his head. "You guys are all right."

Bannon put his arm around Butsko's shoulder. "You're the best fucking master sergeant in the Army, Butsko."

"That's right," said Longtree. "You're a mean, ugly son of a bitch, but I'd follow you anywhere."

Frankie couldn't hold back any longer. "Me too. There's nobody like you, Sarge. You know more about the Army than all those other assholes put together."

It was a strange, emotional moment, because none of the men from the recon platoon had talked to each other this way before. The Marines moved away because they knew something heavy was going down. The men from the recon Platoon all had their arms around each other's shoulders and formed a little circle next to the bar. They thought of all the shit they'd been through together, and of their buddies who'd been cut down by the Japs and shipped back to the States in pine boxes. They realized they were lucky to be in Honolulu together, drinking whiskey, far from the war.

But they were men and couldn't let the closeness between them last too long, because it made them uncomfortable.

"I need another fucking drink," Butsko said, taking his arm off Bannon's shoulder.

"Me too," said Frankie. He looked at his watch. "Shit, man, I got to get me some pussy."

Bannon took his arm off Longtree's shoulder and waved it at the bartender. "One more round!" he shouted.

"Coming up," replied the bartender.

The men looked at each other sheepishly, ashamed by their display of emotion. Butsko decided it was up to him to put everything where it was before they started getting mushy.

"You guys had better stay out of trouble while you're in this town," he said. "If any of you wind up in the stockade, don't expect me to come and get you out. You can fucking rot there for all I care, if you're dumb enough to get caught."

"Don't worry," Bannon told him. "We're not here to look for trouble."

"That's right," Frankie said. "We're just here to look for pussy." He slapped Longtree on the stomach with the back of his hand. "Right, Chief?"

"Fucking A," Longtree replied.

The bartender poured the last round of drinks, and Longtree paid for it. The men raised their glasses in the air.

"Here's to young pussy!" Butsko said.

"I'll drink to that any day," replied Frankie La Barbara.

The men touched glasses and then gulped down the whiskey. They had become so drunk that it didn't even burn anymore when it went down.

FOUR . . .

At seven o'clock in the evening Bannon staggered down a gaudy neon street toward a sign that said CURTIS HOTEL. All around him were bars, shooting galleries, pool halls, and other sleezy waterfront businesses that catered to servicemen. Bannon paused in the doorway of a shoeshine shop and lit an Old Gold cigarette. He spat and shook his head to clear out the sludge of too much drinking. *Jesus, I must look a mess,* he thought.

He took off his cunt cap and smoothed down his sandy hair. Reaching toward his necktie, he tightened the knot and centered it. Looking down, he saw that his uniform was wrinkled but unstained. He'd just had a cup of coffee in a little diner a few blocks away, and it had sobered him up a little. Now all he wanted to do was get his hands on a naked young woman, and the fastest easiest way to do that was to pay for it.

He puffed his cigarette and made his way toward the front of the Curtis Hotel. The air was salty with the smell of the bay not far away, and overlaid with the scent of oil from the ships lying at anchor. Bannon coughed into the back of his hand and took another puff from his cigarette, thinking of the great time

29

he'd had with Butsko and the others at that bar. Back on Guadalcanal he'd never dreamed he'd drink in a bar with them someday, and it had been a blast. Butsko had been great as usual, Frankie had been funny, and Longtree had loosened up for the first time since Bannon had met him. An hour ago they'd all split up to do the things they wanted to do. Bannon had stopped at a pawnshop to buy a cheap switchblade knife, because Butsko told him it got a little tough down on the waterfront, and then he'd headed like a bird dog toward the Curtis Hotel.

He stood underneath the sign and looked at the door, which shimmered before him like Satan's gate. He heard footsteps coming down stairs and stepped out of the way. The door was flung open and two sailors stepped onto the sidewalk, laughing and reeling, their white caps on the backs of their heads and their hair tousled on their foreheads.

"What're the girls like up there?" Bannon asked them.

"Not bad at all," one of them said.

"Ask for Trixie," the other one said. "She's about the best."

"Thanks," said Bannon.

The sailors walked off and Bannon opened the door, looking up at the narrow flight of stairs. It didn't look promising at all. In fact, it was kind of grim, but it was the third week of May and most servicemen were broke toward the end of every month, when they got paid.

At the top of the stairs Bannon pushed open another door and blinked as he stepped into a scene of gaudy elegance. He was in a corridor covered with red wallpaper, and chandeliers hung from the ceiling. The banisters were polished wood and the knobs on the doors that lined the corridor were polished brass.

Across from Bannon was a counter, and behind it were two women and two big guys, who Bannon figured were the bouncers.

"Can I help you, soldier?" asked one of the women, who had curly gray hair and looked like somebody's grandmother.

Bannon didn't know what to say. He'd never seen such a nice-looking old lady in a whorehouse before.

"Can I help you?" she asked again.

Bannon stumbled toward the counter and put out his ciga-

30

rette in the ashtray on the counter. "I hear you got some girls up here," he said.

"Who told you that?" the old lady asked.

"My platoon sergeant."

She looked him over with her sharp twinkling eyes, and so did the bouncers and the other woman, who was Chinese. Maybe they figured he was a cop or an MP, so he thought he'd better set them straight.

"I'm just a regular soldier," he said, "and I'd like to get together with a nice girl."

The old woman smiled. "You came to the right place. What's your name?"

"Bannon."

"Go upstairs and somebody will take care of you," she said, reaching for the telephone.

"Thank you, ma'am."

Bannon turned around and saw the flight of stairs a short distance down the corridor. He walked toward the stairs and climbed them. The red wallpaper beside him was covered with designs in a maroon material that looked like velvet, and he touched it with his fingers as he ascended. It wasn't velvet, but it was something fuzzy that was similar.

He came to the top of the stairs, and his heart sank when he saw a tough-looking middle-aged woman with her brown hair in a shiny curly permanent. *I don't feel like fucking her,* Bannon thought. *I hope they got somebody up here better-looking than her.*

"You, Bannon?" he asked.

"Yes, ma'am."

Her face broke into a big smile. "Well, don't look so scared, honey. I ain't gonna eat you."

Bannon found himself in another corridor like the one downstairs, with the same style wallpaper and the same chandeliers. "Real nice place you got here," he said.

"I'll bet it's a lot better than what you're used to."

"Yes, ma'am."

"You're a southern boy, aren't you?"

"I'm from Texas, ma'am."

"I knew it, because you southern boys are always so polite."

Bannon blushed. "Yes ma'am."

31

She pinched his cheek. "You're real cute too. Come on with me."

"Where *you* from?" he asked, following her down the corridor.

"Seattle."

"I ain't never been to Seattle."

"Well, you ain't missed much."

She stopped in front of a door and opened it up. "Have a seat in there. Can I get you something to drink?"

"Could I get a cup of black coffee, please?"

"Sure thing."

He entered the room and she closed the door behind him. The room was a little bigger than an average hotel room and had upholstered chairs and sofas lining the walls, which were covered with white wallpaper. Pictures in frames were on the walls and the room was illuminated by electric lamps. It looked comfortable and inviting to Bannon, and he sat on a chair in a corner, opposite two soldiers talking to two attractive young women wearing cocktail dresses. The women smiled at him and the guys made believe he wasn't there, because they were a little embarrassed to be seen by a stranger in a whorehouse.

Bannon wasn't embarrassed at all. The way he looked at it, you had to pay for women no matter how you went about it, and some supposedly nice girls were as fussy about how much you spent on them as any whore. On top of that, the nice girls sometimes wouldn't give you any pussy after you spent all the money, but a whore always would, because that was her job. Whores excited Bannon, because they'd do any depraved thing you asked them to do, providing you'd pay.

The two soldiers left with the two whores, and while the door was open the tough-looking woman came in with a little silver pot of coffee, a cup, and a saucer.

"All alone in here, huh?" she asked.

"Yes, ma'am."

"Well, you won't be alone for long." She set down the coffee and cup. "Can I get you anything else?"

"How about a redhead?" Bannon asked.

"Coming up," she replied.

She turned and left the room, and Bannon poured himself a cup of coffee. It was steaming hot, and he raised it to his lips, gingerly taking a sip. He smiled and said "Aaahhh," because it was delicious, not like Army coffee, which had the taste of kerosene. It was so bad, they usually didn't even call it coffee. They called it java or joe or something like that.

He lit another cigarette. Somewhere out in the corridor a girl laughed. Bannon had been in whorehouses before and he knew what the score was. Customers and girls met each other in rooms like this and chatted awhile. When a customer found one he liked he told her so, and she took him to her bedroom, where they talked money and did that good thing. In most places you could get just about anything you were able pay for, including two or three girls in a bed if your tastes ran in that direction. Bannon just wanted one girl in one bed. He wasn't too bizarre when it came to sex.

The door opened and a redhead in a white cocktail dress sashayed into the room. "Are you Bannon?" she asked.

"I sure am."

She looked him up and down and sat beside him. "I bet you're kind of lonely in here."

"Not really."

"Do you want me to leave?"

"No, ma'am."

She smiled and did something with her shoulders that made her boobs wiggle around; her dress had a low V neck and Bannon could see half of them. He figured she was in her late twenties, a few years older than he. She wasn't as pretty as he had hoped for, but she wasn't that bad either.

"Like what you see?" she said with a smile.

"Yes, ma'am."

"My name's Julie."

"Whataya say, Julie. Where you from?"

"Chicago."

"Never been there. Hear it's a big place."

"Where you from?"

"Texas. A small town called Pecos."

"What'd you do before the war."

"I was a cowboy."

"Really?"

"Yup."

"You rode a horses and all that stuff?"

"Yup."

"You married?"

33

"Nope."

"Got a girl back home?"

"Yup."

"Miss her?"

"Yup."

Julie winked. "Is she prettier than me?"

"Nobody's prettier than you, baby."

She laughed. "You might have been a cowboy, but you sure as hell know what to say, don't you?"

Bannon shrugged. "Do I?"

"You sure do, soldier boy." She took his cunt cap off his lap and put it on. "How do I look."

"You look better without it."

"How's your coffee?"

"Real good."

The door opened and three sailors came into the room, accompanied by two girls. The sailors were drunk and talking loudly. The girls twirled the ends of the sailors' black neck-erchiefs and ran their fingers through their hair.

"What a way to make a living," Bannon said.

"What do you mean?"

"Doing what you do."

"It ain't so bad."

"It must be a pain in the ass to go to bed with guys you don't like."

Her smile cracked for a moment, then came back. "I love 'em all," she said.

"Bullshit."

"I do."

"Yeah, sure."

"You wanna go to a room with me?"

"After I finish my coffee."

She looked at her watch. "Okay, take your time."

"If you wanna, you can go sit with those sailors over there. They're short one girl and they look hot to trot."

"What's the matter?" she asked, a hurt tone in her voice. "You don't like me?"

"I love you all," Bannon replied.

"Bullshit," she said.

Bannon laughed, and when he settled down he took another drink of coffee.

• • •

In another part of the whorehouse, Nettie Simmons was in one of the ladies' toilets, applying makeup to her face. She'd just finished screwing a Marine and she felt as if she'd been wrestling for the championship of the world. He was a big guy and she was a little female, five feet three inches tall, with long brown hair and a cute little upturned nose. She didn't feel as if she had the strength to handle another serviceman, but it was early in the evening and she didn't go off duty until four in the morning.

She wore a dark blue silk dress, cut low in the front like all the dresses the girls had to wear, and she had big boobs for a girl her size. She was twenty-three years old and had low self-esteem, which was why she was a whore.

Leaving the toilet, she walked down the corridor and saw Mae, the tough-looking brunette.

"Which room?" asked Nettie.

"That one over there—and smile, for Chrissakes."

"I'll smile when I get into the room," Nettie said.

True to her word, she opened the door and smiled. Patti and LouAnn were talking with two sailors, and Julie was with a tall soldier who wore the combat infantryman's badge on his shirt. Nettie always tried to be extra nice to the combat veterans, because she figured they needed her most. He was a nice-looking fellow, real tall, with long legs, light hair, and deeply tanned skin. She walked across the room and sat down on the other side of him.

"Hi," she said. "What's going on?"

"Meet Bannon," said Julie. "He's from Texas."

"No kidding," said Nettie. "I bet you rode a lot of horses in your day," she told Bannon.

"That ain't all I rode," Bannon replied with a wink.

Well, he sure ain't shy, Nettie thought. "My name's Nettie."

"Whataya say, Nettie. You from Kentucky?"

"South Carolina."

"I thought I heard some cornpone and hushpuppies coming out of your mouth."

"Why sho' 'nuff," she said, going along with the gag.

Bannon looked at her and tried to figure out whether she was pretty or not. With most girls he could tell right off the bat. Either they were or they weren't. But Nettie was a flawed beauty, or at least that's what he thought at first. Her nose was a little too small and turned up too much, and her chin wasn't well formed—it didn't cut back sharply enough—but it wasn't a double-chin either. Bannon narrowed his eyes as he examined her. *Maybe she is beautiful,* he thought, reconsidering. *She's just got a look that's all her own.*

"You don't like me," she said, her voice falling.

"No, I do like you."

Julie cleared her throat. "Don't worry about it," she said to Nettie, "he doesn't like me either."

"That's not so," Bannon said, taking out a cigarette. "I like you both."

"Liar," said Nettie. "Well, I think I'm gonna talk to that sailor over there."

Bannon grabbed her wrist and was surprised at how slim it was. She was like a little doll, except for her hefty tits. "No, stick around."

"What for? You don't like me."

"Yes I do."

"No you don't."

"What do I have to do to prove it to you."

She smiled, and he felt his heart melting away. "You know what to do."

"Okay," Bannon said, "let's go."

Julie leaned back in her chair. "Well, I'll be damned."

Nettie's smile broadend. She looked like a little girl who'd just been given a box of candy. She stood pertly and held out her hand to him. "C'mon."

Bannon gulped down the rest of his coffee and stood beside her. He was six feet tall and she barely came up to his chest. She was like a child, except for those boobs and a certain wickedness around her mouth and eyes. He thought she was very intriguing and strange. Part of him wanted to protect her, and the other part wanted to fuck her brains out.

She led him out of the room and into the corridor, where Mae smiled at them. Bannon threw her a salute with one finger; his mind was still a little pickled by all the drinking he'd done. He walked down the corridor hand in hand with Nettie and felt ludicrous, because they were behaving like lovers going to their hotel room instead of a whore and a horny GI on the way to a business transaction.

Her hand was small and frail, like a little bird. He bent down and smelled the fragrance of her hair. She walked gracefully, with her head held high, and he thought there was something precious and sweet about her. His heart beat faster. He felt dizzy and confused.

"In here," she said.

She took a key out of her pocketbook and opened the door of a room that looked like a basic hotel room. It had a bed, dresser, chair, and a big mirror hanging over the dresser. On top of the dresser were bottles of cosmetics. She closed the door and placed her purse on the dresser.

"Well," she said, "what do you want?"

He puffed his cigarette and felt awkward, which surprised him because he usually wasn't awkward around whores. But this one was making him feel as if he were doing something wrong. "I don't know," he said. "What do things cost?"

"Five dollars for a straight fuck, seven-fifty for a half-and-half, and ten dollars for a full blowjob."

"How much time I get?"

"As much as you need."

"How much is that, usually."

"How much time do you need, usually?"

Bannon shrugged. "I dunno—I never timed it." He reached into his pocket and took out his roll of bills. He peeled off two tens and handed them to her. "I guess this ought to hold us for a while."

She stared at the bills with her big brown eyes. "Sure will." She scooped them up with her elegant fingers. "I'll be right back. You can take your clothes off."

She left the room, her silk dress rustling, and Bannon flicked his cigarette ash into an ashtray. He set his cunt cap on the dresser and looked at himself in the mirror: He was bleary-eyed and a little wasted. He unknotted his necktie, pulled it off, and dropped it on his cunt cap. Then he unbuttoned his shirt. The chain that held his dogtags showed against his tanned chest.

Nettie returned to the room. "You're not undressed yet?"

"Nope."

"I won't hurry you. This is a slow night here. Usually is toward the end of the month."

She tugged something at her side and her cocktail dress fell away. She hung it over a chair; she was naked underneath. Bannon's hand froze on his shirt button as he stared at her. Her boobs stood right up there all by themselves, she had a terrific ass, and her legs were muscular and powerful. She was a strange, beautiful combination of fragility and strength.

She acted shy and coy. "Ain't you ever seen a naked girl before?"

"Lots of times."

"Well, stop looking at me like that. You're making me nervous. You look like you want to eat me up alive."

"Baby, I'd love to eat you up alive."

"I wouldn't want anybody to eat me up alive. That must be the worst thing in the world that could happen to a person."

"I wasn't talking about chewing you up and swallowing you down. I didn't mean it that way."

"Well, that's the way it sounded."

She stood in front of the mirror and fluffed her hair out with the backs of her hands. He sat on the chair and took off his shoes and socks. Then he stood and dropped his pants and shorts. She walked across the room to the sink and turned on the water.

"Come on over here," she said.

Bannon crossed the room and stood beside her. The fragrance from her hair was wonderful. He didn't feel very lustful, and thought maybe he should have picked another whore. This one was pretty enough, but there also was something innocent about her that made him think of her as his kid sister. Yet, she was naked as a jaybird and had those great tits and that ass that wouldn't quit. It was very unsettling.

"Lemme look at you," she said.

She dropped to one knee in front of him, held his cock in her fist, and squeezed it, examining the head.

"You don't have a disease, do you?"

"Nope."

She looked his joint over, scratching here and there, wrinkling her nose, twisting it around so she could see its underside.

"You look okay," she said, standing up. "Come on closer to the sink."

He stood closer and she filled the bowl with warm water. She dipped her hands in the water, lathered her hands with soap, and then washed his cock. The slippery, smooth sensation felt good, and it turned Bannon on. His cock began to get hard.

"There you go," she said, looking down at her handiwork proudly. "You know, you're a real nice-looking feller. Some of the guys who come in here really aren't that nice-looking."

"It must be awful, screwing guys you don't like."

"It's my job."

"Why don't you get another job?"

"Let's change the subject."

"Okay."

She rinsed the soap off his cock, massaging it gently with her hands; he was as hard as a rock.

"Where'd you get that scar on your side?" she asked.

"That's where the bayonet went in."

"Jesus."

She pulled his cock out of the basin and dried it off with a fresh towel. She was being very diligent and thorough, and it made him sad. She was really a nice girl, very conscientious about her lousy job, and she shouldn't be there.

"You shouldn't be here," he said.

"What do you mean?"

"Working in a whorehouse."

"I said I don't wanna talk about that. Lie down on the bed."

He walked across the room to the bed. She pulled down the bedspread and exposed the gleaming white sheets. *They must change the sheets after every fuck,* he thought. Butsko was right. This really was a very nice whorehouse.

He lay down on his back, and she climbed onto the bed, perching between his legs. She took his cock in her hand, jerked him off a few times, then bent over and put it in her mouth. Bannon placed his hands behind his head and looked down at her. He thought her very beautiful and lovely, and there she was, sucking his cock like a good little girl because it was her job. A lot of whores—in fact, nearly all whores—didn't care at all. They just went through the motions once you paid them. But this little one was trying hard. She was a good kid, and he felt sorry for her. This was what she did every day—sucking the cocks of drunken servicemen. This was her life. How could she do it?

39

And yet, with his feelings of sympathy for her, she was making him very excited. She was a skillful cocksucker and her eyes were bright, as if she were enjoying it. Her head bobbed around and her boobs jangled up and down. Her long brown hair, which nearly extended to her waist, went thrashing through the air. She was like a little doll; everything about her was exquisite, and he even thought that her small upturned nose was perfect for her face now, and that her chin had the most alluring shape.

And she was completely in his power. He paid for her and could do anything with her he liked. If he told her to do it, she had to do it—within reason, of course. Now he wanted to feel her against him. He wanted to kiss her demure lips, even though she'd probably sucked a hundred cocks that day. He didn't care. He hadn't had a woman since the native girl, and he hadn't had her for a couple of months.

He placed both of his hands on her head and pushed her up off him.

She blinked and was disconcerted. "Am I doing something wrong?"

"Come on up here," he said softly, pulling her toward him.

She climbed up his body and he held her cheeks in his hands, looking at her face, and her lips were red due to the exertion and friction they'd been undergoing.

"You know, you're really okay," he said.

She smiled. "I was afraid I was doing something wrong."

"Naw, you couldn't do anything wrong."

He pulled her face closer to him and they kissed gently. Her lips and tongue were hot and had a sweet taste. He removed his hands from her cheeks and ran them down her back, bringing them to rest on her buns.

"You got a great little figure," he said.

"Thanks. You got a great body yourself."

He was going to say *I bet you say that to all the soldiers*, but he didn't because he knew she didn't. There was something honest about her. She wouldn't tell lies unless she had to, and then she'd tell them poorly.

"I wish I would've met you someplace else," he said.

She snickered. "If you woulda met me someplace else, you wouldn't be fucking me."

"That's okay."

"Yeah?"

"Yeah."

She jabbed her fingers into his ribs. "You're fulla shit—that's what you are. You just trying to get under my skin—that's what you're trying to do."

"I'm telling you the truth, baby."

"Sure you are."

"Why don't you believe me?"

"Why should I believe you? I always get suspicious when people start telling me to believe them. I know they're about to tell me a whopper."

"You think that if I met you outside of here I wouldn't like you?"

"Sure you would. You probably want to stick this thing here into every girl you see, from eight to eighty, blind, crippled, or crazy." She took his cock in her hand and moved it toward her magic place.

"Not every girl."

"Most every girl." She tucked it inside her warmth. "How does that feel?"

"Like I died and went to heaven."

She chuckled. "You sure talk a good game, soldier."

"It's the truth."

She moved his cock until it was at the proper angle and then pushed her pelvis forward, enveloping him with her vagina. It was greasy and snug, and thrills went up and down his spine.

"Aaaaahhhh," he said.

"Feels good, huh?"

"Yeah."

"How about this?"

She rocked up and down on him and giggled when she saw the expression on his face. She pressed her forefinger against his nose.

"You're just a big baby, ain'tcha?"

She kissed his forehead, his eyes, the tip of his nose, and his lips. Then she hunkered down, ran her tongue over his nipples, and worked him slowly. He looked down at the top of her head and cupped her ass in his hands. It was firm and

41

strong, not soft and flabby, like some girls'. She wiggled from side to side and brought her legs close together, which caused her vagina to squeeze his cock.

"Come for me, baby," she whispered. "Go ahead and do it."

He didn't want to come so soon, but he knew if she kept doing what she was doing, he would before long. She slurped all over his chest as she worked her hips around and about.

"Want me to suck it again for you?" she asked.

He didn't answer, because he was getting sex-crazy. He wanted to squeeze her hard but was afraid he'd break her little bones. He wanted to take a bite right out of her shoulder.

He clasped her tightly against him and moved to the side so he could get on top of her.

"Wheeeeee!" she cried happily.

He laid her on her back, wrapped his arms around her, and started long-stroking. She clasped her legs around him and wiggled from side to side.

"Fuck me, Daddy," she whispered into his ear. "Fuck me all night long."

He pumped her from all the angles, swiveling his hips, going out of his mind. She met him stroke for stroke, and in his delirium he was amazed at how strong she was for such a little girl. He held her head in his hands and thrust his tongue into her mouth, and she wrapped her tongue around it, sucking gently, coaxing him to a higher level of wild passion. He humped her passionately and she dug her fingernails into his shoulders, matching his rhythm and intensity.

The bed creaked and squeaked, and both of them breathed heavily, gulping down air as if they were running a marathon and had only a few hundred more yards to go. He moved his hands down her body and grabbed her ass again, pulling her toward him, and she tangled her fingers in his hair and pulled his lips more tightly against hers.

He felt himself coming and tried to prolong it. He closed his eyes and tried to think of the Texas prairies on a hot afternoon, the sun beating on his ten-gallon hat and the cattle munching grass. But it did no good. She pushed his face away and grit her teeth, moving her head from side to side on the pillow,

42

saying "ooh" and "aahh," and when he looked down at her, he could see that her eyes showed mostly white because they were rolled up into her head.

His balls exploded, and he bucked like a wild bronco. The bed bounced up and down on the floor as he shot his first load into her, and she screamed into his ear so loudly it shocked him. But he couldn't stop moving and continued to pump her, jolting and pushing, hanging on tightly as he shot fusillade after fusillade into her.

In a sudden weird movement she reached up and bit his chin, but he barely felt it because he was drowning in ecstasy. He gasped for breath as she fell away from him, sweat coating both of their bodies, semen soaking the sheets underneath her ass. He blacked out for a few seconds and came back again, still humping that little girl underneath him. And she wouldn't quit, either; she just kept wiggling and twisting, pushing back at him, and her little pussy squeezed his cock like a fist.

Finally he simply couldn't move anymore, and collapsed on top of her. She went limp, and he felt her chest rise and fall as she tried to breathe.

"You son of a bitch," she said. "You made me come."

"Don't gimme that," he said.

"You did!"

"I did?"

She slapped his ass. "You damn sure did."

"Oh, baby," he said, and kissed her cheek, her nose, and her throat. Huffing and puffing, he slithered down her body and kissed her healthy breasts, sucking the nipples, feasting on her. But his energy was dribbling out of him and he couldn't go on. He lay his head between her breasts and stopped moving. Underneath his ear he could hear her heart beating like a tom-tom.

He struggled to catch his breath, and so did she. He thought of how strange it was to be in bed with a girl. On Guadalcanal he thought about sex nearly all the time; it seemed like the most exotic and wonderful thing in the world, but now as he lay in bed with this little whore he realized how natural sex was, how he used to do this all the time when he was a civilian, and how important it was for a man's mental health.

It had been a great fuck too. One of the best in his life. She really was something, perfect in every way. The man who married her would be a lucky son of a bitch. He'd have a hot piece of ass for the rest of his life.

"You're really special," he whispered into her boobs. "You're so pretty and nice and sweet, and you're really a terrific lay. You're like a magic princess, and I don't think I've ever met anybody like you."

She groaned. "Guys tell me that all the time."

He was astounded because he thought he was the only one. He'd figured that the other guys just got on her, fucked her, came, and walked out the door. He had been certain no one had ever said such nice things to her, but now he realized he was just another john.

Just another john.

Shit.

He got up on his elbows and looked down bitterly at her.

"What's the matter with you?" she asked.

"Never mind."

He crawled off the bed, took his pack of cigarettes out of his shirt, and popped one into his mouth. He plucked his Zippo out of his pants and lit the cigarette, then reached for his skivvies and put them on.

"Hey," she said, "you don't have to leave yet."

He buttoned up his skivvies, then picked up his pants and put them on.

"You mad or something?" she asked.

"No."

"Yes you are."

"Well, maybe I am."

"How come."

"Never mind."

"We can do it again if you want to."

"Forget it." He sat on the chair and reached for his khaki socks, feeling humiliated and cheap. *I'm just a fucking john,* he thought.

She adjusted the pillow against the headboard and rested her head against it, bending her legs that her knees pointed into the air. "I know what's eating you," she said. "You're mad because I told you that other guys say the same things to me that you say. Well, they do. I just said the truth and you

44

can't take it. Everybody tells me how pretty I am, but nobody wants to do anything about it."

"Like what?"

"You know like what."

"No I don't."

"Yes you do."

"You mean like marry you or something?"

She didn't say anything.

"I just asked you a question, goddammit!"

She looked at him angrily. "Don't you holler at me, soldier boy. I'm not one of your damned recruits."

She rolled out of bed, tiptoed to her dress, and took her own pack of cigarettes out of its folds. She put one in her mouth, lit it with a match, and tiptoed to the sink, turning on the faucets.

"I'll wash you off if you're finished," she said, very businesslike.

"I don't need it."

"Suit yourself."

She straddled the sink and washed her vagina. Bannon tied his shoelaces and stood, picking his shirt off the chair.

"I bet all the guys make you come too," he said sarcastically.

"No," she replied. "That almost never happens."

"You little fucking liar!" he said.

"Why would I lie to you about one thing and not the other?" she asked. "Use your head, soldier boy."

He wrinkled his forehead, because that made sense. If she was going to lie to him, she would have lied straight across the board. He looked at her; she was even smaller in her bare feet, patting her groin with the towel. Her makeup had come off in the lovemaking, and she looked like the country girl that she really was.

"How long you been a whore?" he asked, putting on his shirt.

"None of your business."

"You know what you're gonna look like after another couple years, don't you?"

She shrugged. "Who cares."

"You're gonna care."

"Don't tell me what I'm gonna do, soldier boy. You don't

45

know nothing about me at all."

"Shit," Bannon said, "I can just look at you and tell you where you've been, where you are now, and where you're going."

"I don't wanna hear it."

"You're gonna wind up like all them old toothless whores standing on street corners, blowing guys for quarters."

"I said I don't wanna hear it."

She walked across the room, a scowl on her face, put her feet into her high-heeled shoes, and lifted her blue silk dress off the chair. She put the dress on, zipped up the side, and suddenly she was dressed again.

"Why don't you get an honest job?" he asked, tucking in his shirt. "There's a million defense jobs out there, and they pay good money."

"Not as good as this," she said.

"You can't do this forever."

"After I get enough money saved I'm gonna go back home and start a business."

"That's what all the whores say, and they all wind up on street corners, blowing guys for quarters."

She stood in front of the mirror and brushed out her long brown hair.

"Why don't you get married?" he said.

"Who the hell would marry me?" she replied.

"I'd marry you."

He looked at him sharply. "Liar."

"I'm not a liar."

"You're so full of shit it's coming out of your ears." She turned to the mirror again and continued brushing her hair.

"I bet a lot of guys would marry you."

"A lot of guys would say that so they could get some free pussy for a while, and then when the time came they wouldn't."

"That ever happen to you?"

"Button your lip, soldier boy. You don't have the right to talk to me like this just because you paid twenty dollars."

"I'll marry you right fucking today!" he said.

"I said button your fat lip."

"C'mon, I'll prove it." He took a step toward her. "We'll find a justice of the peace and get married."

46

She gave him a dirty look, put a hairpin in her mouth, and continued brushing her hair.

Bannon tied on his necktie and stood behind her so he could see in the mirror that it was straight. Their eyes met in the mirror; hers were smoldering with anger. She put the pin into her hair, then bent forward and picked up her lipstick.

Bannon looked at the outline of her ass against the silk dress. She was pretty and nice, even though she was being contrary. He wanted her to lead a normal life and be happy.

He grabbed her arm. "C'mon, let's get married right now."

She pulled her arm away. "Take your paws off me!"

He grabbed her arm again. "If you don't come with me, you're just going to be a whore all your life."

She tried to pull away, but this time he held her too tightly.

"I'll marry you," he said evenly, looking into her eyes. "You'll get my Army allotment and you won't even have to work at anything if you don't want to."

She tore her eyes from his and looked down at his hand clenched around her arm. "Let me go!"

"I won't let you go. We're getting married. If you're not smart enough to lead a normal life, I'll go goddamn make you."

"Like hell you will!" she said, tugging to get away.

He held her more tightly. "Listen, you know you like me. We'd get along fine, and I won't even be around that much. I'll be away in the war. Be a person for a change, instead of the girl who has to suck everybody's cock for ten dollars."

Her eyes welled up and darted around like the eyes of a frightened animal. *"Let me go!"* she screamed.

"Trust me," he said. "Just walk out this door with me and trust me."

"Why should I trust you?" she shrieked. "Who are you? You're just another soldier boy with a smooth line of shit!"

"I'm not!" he said, pulling her toward the door. "I'm going to marry you right fucking now to prove it!"

"Let me go!"

"No!"

"Help!"

"Ssshhh!" he said, placing his forefinger in front of his lips. "Calm down."

"Heeellllppp!"

Becoming angry, he pushed her against the wall, a little harder than he'd intended. "You're too fucking dumb to know what's good for you!" he shouted.

The door to the room opened suddenly and Mae burst in. Behind her were a few other women. They took a look at Nettie up against the wall and Bannon standing menacingly in front of her.

"What the hell's going on here?" Mae asked.

"This son of a bitch is crazy!" Nellie shouted.

Mae looked at Bannon. "Now, you just take it easy, soldier."

"I am taking it easy," Bannon replied, trying to take it easy.

"I think," Mae said, "that you'd better just turn around and walk out of here, soldier."

"I ain't going anywhere without her." He looked at Nettie cringing against the wall and held out his hand. "Come on, girl. Take a chance."

"Get the hell away from me!" she screamed.

"Soldier," said Mae, "you can see that she doesn't want to go. Why don't you leave her alone?"

"I ain't leaving her here."

"Come on," Mae said with a soothing tone in her voice. "Go back to Schofield Barracks and sleep it off."

Bannon looked at Nettie. "You don't have to be a whore," he said. "Come with me and I'll marry you, I swear."

Nettie bit her lower lip and looked away from him. She didn't say a word. There was a commotion in the hall and then the nice old lady who'd been at the desk downstairs entered the room, followed by the two big bouncers.

"What's the problem?" she asked, for she was the madam of the whorehouse.

"This soldier is acting up," Mae said.

The little old lady placed her hands on her hips and walked toward Bannon, her eyes like the slits in the turret of a tank. "Mister, we don't want any trouble here. I think you ought to go home right now."

"I ain't leaving without her," Bannon replied. "She wants to come with me, but she's just a little scared, that's all."

"I don't want to go anywhere with you!" Nettie screamed. *"You're a crazy son of a bitch!"*

"You heard her," the madam said. "She don't wanna go

anywhere with you. You're a little out of line. Why don't you just walk out of here and we'll forget about everything."

Bannon turned and looked at Nettie. "I'm going through a lot of trouble for you. Now, come on, goddammit!"

"You're not doing anything for me!" she shrieked. "You're just doing it for yourself!"

"Come on, soldier!" said the madam. "Why don't you leave under your own steam while you've got the chance?"

"I ain't leaving without Nettie."

"I ain't gonna ask you again."

"Come on, Nettie," Bannon pleaded. "I'll make an honest woman out of you."

"I am an honest woman!" Nettie hollered.

"Soldier," said the madam, "this is your last chance."

"Listen, Nettie," Bannon said, "just put one foot in front of the other one and follow me."

"No!"

The madam got out of the way and the two bouncers stepped forward. The one on the left wore a gray suit that was too tight for him, and the one on the right had on a shirt without a tie and the sleeves rolled up, showing massive hairy arms.

"Let's go, feller," the one on the left said, holding out his hand to grab Bannon's arm.

Bannon jumped back out of range like a cat. He crouched down and looked at the two bouncers as they approached him cautiously.

"Somebody call the cops," the madam said, and one of the girls in the doorway ran off down the corridor.

The bouncers moved toward Bannon. "Don't make it hard on yourself," the one in the suit said. He had cauliflower ears and had probably been a prizefighter. "Don't make us get tough with you."

The bouncers were big tough guys, but they didn't know who they were messing with. Bannon had been in hundreds of hand-to-hand fights with Japanese soldiers on Guadalcanal, and violence was as natural to him as fucking was to a whore.

"You lay a hand on me," Bannon said, "and it'll be your ass."

"Come on," the bouncer in the suit said. "Let's hit the road."

The bouncer laid his hand on Bannon's shoulder and, quick as a cat, Bannon ducked under his hand and punched him with

49

all his strength in the stomach. Bannon's fist went in almost to the wrist, and the bouncer said "oof," bending over. Bannon hit him with an uppercut that straightened him out and sent him flying against the wall. He crashed against the wall and sank down, dazed.

One of the women handed a billy club to the other bouncer, the one wearing the shirt with the sleeves rolled up.

"Don't make me use this," the bouncer said, holding the club in his fist with the end pointing at the ceiling.

"Put that thing away or I'll make you eat it," Bannon said.

"Soldier boy, you're getting to be a real pain in the ass around here."

Bannon turned to Nettie. "You can still come out of here with me."

"You can go straight to hell!"

The bouncer swung down the billy club, and Bannon reached up and grabbed his wrist, stopping it in midair; at the same time he kneed the bouncer in the balls. The bouncer moaned and sank to his knees, clutching his groin with both hands. Bannon kicked him in the chops and sent him reeling backward.

Women screamed, holding their fists against their ears. Bannon lunged toward Nettie and grabbed her wrist.

"You're coming with me!" he said.

She didn't say anything because she was scared to death. Bannon pulled her toward the door, but meanwhile the bouncer in the suit had picked himself off the floor and lurched in front of the door to block Bannon's way.

"Hold it right there," said the bouncer, his lip bleeding from where Bannon hit him with the uppercut.

"If you don't get out of my way, I'm gonna go right the fuck over you," Bannon told him, holding Nettie tightly.

"Oh, yeah?"

The bouncer reached into his pocket and pulled out a switch-blade knife. He hit the button and the blade snapped out. He held the knife with his thumb on the blade and the blade pointing straight up in the air.

"Put that knife away!" the madam yelled.

The bouncer looked at Bannon and turned down the corners of his mouth. "Soldier boy, you fucked with the wrong guy. I'm gonna cut you up."

Bannon saw the knife flashing in the light of the electric

lamps and didn't take his eyes off it. He let go of Nettie, who ran to a corner and leaned against it, her face as white as the wallpaper. Bannon reached into his pocket and took out the cheap switchblade he'd bought at the pawnshop earlier in the day. He pushed his thumbnail against the safety and pressed the button. The blade opened out with a loud clack and Bannon waved it from side to side in the air while he spread his legs apart and got set.

"Come on, motherfucker," Bannon said. "Cut me up."

Bannon shifted his weight from one foot to the other as the bouncer advanced stealthily, light on his feet for such a bulky man. Bannon moved to his right and they began to circle each other. The bouncer feinted with his knife, and Bannon adjusted his posture to meet the thrust that never came. Bannon feinted and the bouncer raised his free hand. They continued to circle each other. The room was so quiet that the breathing of Bannon and the bouncer could be heard, along with the terrified gasps of little Nettie. Bannon and the bouncer were both big men, although the bouncer was bigger, and both felt at home with knives in their hands, but there was one fundamental difference between them: The bouncer had never killed anyone in his life, and Bannon had killed many men. Bannon knew that fights with knives usually ended quickly after somebody made the first move. As he circled the bouncer he wondered whether to make the first move himself and have the advantage of surprise on his side, or entice the bouncer to make the first move, which would leave the bouncer open for a stab.

The bouncer feinted suddenly and Bannon stepped backward, but then the bouncer thrust his knife forward, directly at Bannon's stomach, and Bannon dodged to the side, the bouncer's knife slicing empty air.

"I'm over here," Bannon said with a grim smile.

The bouncer turned to face him. Sweat ran down the bouncer's face and covered the top of his head, which was bald. Bannon's sudden move surprised the bouncer and rattled his confidence. He knew now that Bannon was faster than he, but he was sure he was stronger. If he could get close to Bannon, he thought he could muscle him and stick his knife in a soft spot.

The bouncer had been a boxer, and he knew that when you fight a man faster than you, the only thing to do is cut off the ring and get in close so you can pound his guts out. He thought the same principle would apply to Bannon, so instead of circling he switched direction and tried to get closer, confident he could grab Bannon's knife hand and then push his own knife into Bannon's heart.

Bannon moved the other way and the bouncer changed direction again, moving closer. Bannon switched again and the bouncer reached out suddenly to grab Bannon's wrist, but his big hand closed on thin air, and in the next second he felt a horrible tearing pain in his stomach, a pain so overwhelming that his knees buckled and he nearly passed out.

Bannon pulled his switch out of the bouncer's gut as the screams of the women echoed in his ears. He reared his arm back and slashed through the air, severing the bouncer's windpipe and jugular vein, blood spurting onto the rug.

The bouncer collapsed at Bannon's feet and lay still, blood pouring out his neck and throat. The women were hysterical and Bannon knew he was in a whole world of trouble. He took his handkerchief out of his pocket and wiped off the knife, then dropped it onto the dead body of the bouncer.

Meanwhile the women wept and slobbered, hugging each other, certain he was a madman who would massacre them all. But Bannon was as calm and cool as he was when in combat.

"Get away from the door!" he commanded.

The women near the door whimpered and fled to both sides of the room, shivering, holding their hands to their mouths. Bannon turned around and looked at Nettie, who was sitting on the floor, staring into space like a soldier who'd been shelled for forty-eight hours. Bannon didn't say anything to her, because there was nothing left to say.

He walked to the door, opened it up and stepped into the hall. He heard footsteps coming up stairs. *The roof,* he thought, *I've got to get up there.* He ran toward the stairs and jumped up several of them, then realized that people were coming down the stairs also. He recalled that someone had been sent to call the police earlier. They must be closing in on him.

He ran back to the room, and the women screamed again. They were bending over the body of the bouncer, and they scattered as Bannon leaped over the bed and landed next to the window. He opened it up and looked outside. There was no fire escape, only a three-story drop, and just then the alley below filled up from both ends with uniformed cops who had their guns out.

Bannon spun around and heard footsteps in the corridor outside. He'd left the door open and realized that had been a mistake. He stomped toward the dead body of the bouncer and picked up his switchblade, because when combat soldiers are in trouble they tend to pick up weapons.

A cop appeared in the doorway, looked at Bannon, saw the knife in his hand, thought for a moment that it was a gun, and nearly shot him down. But before his finger could move the final eighth of an inch on the trigger, he realized it was only a knife.

The cop entered the room, followed by other cops. They were swarthy-skinned Hawaiians and looked scared to death.

"Drop that knife!" one of the cops said.

Bannon looked at the barrels of all the guns pointing to him and knew he didn't have a chance. He dropped the knife and it clattered onto the floor.

"Hold your hands over your head!"

Bannon raised his hands over his head and two cops rushed toward him, slapping him down for concealed weapons.

"He's clean," one of them said.

"Cuff him."

"Hold out your hands!" a cop said to Bannon.

Bannon held out his hands and the cop snapped the cuffs on. The cop grabbed Bannon by the collar of his shirt and pushed him toward the door. Bannon turned around and saw Nettie sitting on the floor, looking at him. Their eyes met and Bannon wanted to say something clever, but he couldn't think of anything.

The cop pushed Bannon into the corridor, full of cops staring and aiming their guns at him.

"You're under arrest!" he heard a voice say.

The cops gathered around Bannon and dragged him toward the stairs.

FIVE . . .

The taxicab turned the corner and drove down a quiet residential street on the outskirts of Honolulu. Butsko sat in the backseat, smoking a cigarette, looking at the one-story stucco homes that lined the street. It was night, and lights shone through the windows of the homes, while street lamps lit their facades. It wasn't a fancy or expensive neighborhood, and on front lawns were kids' tricycles, broken dolls, and cars that had been cannibalized for parts to keep other cars going. It all looked familiar to Butsko, because he'd lived with Dolly on this street until they broke up nearly two years earlier.

Halfway down the street Butsko heard blaring music. It was a recording of one of the big bands; he couldn't identify which one because he wasn't up on things like that.

"Which house?" asked the driver.

"A little farther down the block, on the right."

Butsko took a drag from his cigarette and blew the smoke out the side of his mouth. This street had been full of cop cars on the night he punched Dolly out. Oh, what a scene that had been. They'd taken him away in a paddy wagon and locked him in the Honolulu jail, and then he was transferred to the

Schofield Barracks post stockade. Dolly went to the hospital to have her jaw wired up. *I really shouldn't be coming back here,* Butsko told himself, but he couldn't help it. He'd fought with himself but he'd lost. Something was pulling him out here and he was going along with it. *Maybe I'm still in love with the bitch*—I don't know.

The music became louder as Butsko approached his house, and he realized that that was where it was coming from. All the lights were on in the house: Dolly must be having a party. Dolly always loved parties.

"Stop right over there," Butsko said.

"You got it, Sarge."

The cabdriver veered to the right, coasted a few feet, and applied the brakes. The taxicab stopped in front of Butsko's old house.

"Three-eighty," said the cabdriver.

Butsko reached into his pocket and took out his roll of bills. He looked at the house, and something told him not to go in. If Dolly was having a party, she probably had some guys there, and Butsko might be tempted to punch one of them in the mouth.

"I said three-eighty," the cabdriver said. He was a little old Chinese man.

"I heard you," Butsko said. "I'm thinking."

The cabdriver wanted to get nasty, but Butsko was a big ugly man and the cabdriver didn't want any trouble. He looked in the rearview mirror at Butsko gazing at the house.

I really should tell the driver to take me back to town, Butsko thought. *There's nothing in there for me but trouble.*

But then he heard a woman's loud, raucous laughter above the music; he'd know that laugh anywhere. It was Dolly having a good time. On his allotment. In the house he'd put a down payment on. With some other guy.

Butsko became mad. He felt as if Dolly were making a fool out of him. The least he could do was let her know that she wasn't making a fool out of him. In fact, he ought to tell her that he was going to see a lawyer the next day about divorcing her ass. That ought to stop the bitch from laughing.

Butsko gave a five-dollar bill to the cabdriver. "Keep the change, Charlie."

"My name not Charlie."

Butsko pushed open the door and stepped onto the sidewalk. He threw his cigarette butt down, stomped on it, and hiked up his pants. He still was a little woozy from the drinks he'd had with his men. It had been a lot of fun, but they'd better not act too chummy with him when they got back to Guadalcanal, because a platoon sergeant can't be effective if he's too chummy with his men. You've got to keep them afraid of you and kick ass whenever they get out of line.

The cab drove away and Butsko walked toward the front door of his house. He heard the music and sound of voices, male and female. That fucking Dolly. Throwing parties on his allotment while he was getting shot by at the Japs. It was enough to piss a man off.

Butsko walked up to the front door and pounded his fist on it. He waited a few seconds and nothing happened, so he pounded again. The music and chatter continued and he decided he wasn't knocking loud enough, so he reared back his fist and really hammered hard, nearly putting his hand through the door.

A few seconds later the door opened up and a staff sergeant stood there, a glass in his hand. Behind the staff sergeant Butsko could see people dancing.

"Who're you?" the staff sergeant asked, squinting his eyes at Butsko.

"This is my fucking house!" Butsko said. "Who're *you*?"

The staff sergeant blinked. "Whataya mean, this is your house?"

"Get outta my way!"

Butsko pushed him to the side and entered his living room. Men and women were everywhere, dancing and talking, holding glasses. Most of them wore uniforms and everyone looked at him with question marks in their eyes. Just then Dolly entered the room through another door, carrying a bottle of whiskey, and when she looked at Butsko she stopped cold, turned green, and dropped the bottle.

A sailor with fast reflexes dived toward the floor and caught it before it broke. Dolly stared at Butsko for a few moments, and he stared at her. She wore a bright red dress and had gained weight since he had seen her last. Her brown hair was curled and waved in an imitation movie-star glamor hairdo. All conversation stopped and somebody lifted the needle off the record. Dolly pulled herself together and put her hands on her hips.

"What the hell are you doing here?" she said.

"This is my fucking house!" Butsko replied. "What are all *these people* doing here?"

She pointed her finger at him. "You can't come here! I got a court order out on you!"

"Shove it up your ass!" Butsko said.

A Marine taller than Butsko and nearly as broad, with gunnery sergeant stripes on his sleeves, stepped away from the wall. "This guy giving you some trouble, Dolly?"

Butsko looked at the Marine and narrowed his eyes. *Who is this scumbag?* he thought. He thought he knew. The Marine was probably Dolly's boyfriend or had aspirations in that direction. The Marine looked like he could handle himself, but Butsko was sure he could whip his ass.

Dolly looked at both of them and knew a war was about to start in her living room unless she cooled things out. Moreoever, she was living comfortably thanks to Butsko's allotment, and she didn't want to antagonize him if she didn't have to.

"Well," she said, clasping her hands together and smiling broadly at Butsko, "you took me by surprise, Johnny. I haven't seen you for so long, after all." She walked towards him, playing the gracious hostess, and held out her hand. "You're always welcome here, Johnny. Let's let bygones be bygones— what the hell."

She took his hand and squeezed it. This was the one contingency he wasn't prepared for. He was ready to argue with her or beat the shit out of the Marine, but he didn't know what to do now, because deep in his heart he still loved the bitch, despite everything.

"Yeah—okay," he said nervously. "Sure thing."

She could see that she'd caught him off guard, and her confidence returned. She'd always been able to handle the big lug before, except for the time he found her in bed with Sergeant Steeley, but nobody could hope to handle a man in those circumstances.

"What're you drinking, Johnny?"

"Gin."

"How could I forget?"

"I can tell you how you could forget."

She ignored the remark and said expansively: "Folks, I'd

like you to meet my husband, Johnny Butsko."

Everyone stared as she took his arm and pulled him to the table where the bottles and glasses were. She lifted one of the glasses. "Straight up, right?"

"Right."

"Tell me when."

She picked up a bottle of Fleischmann's whisky and poured it into the glass.

"That's enough," he said when it was half full.

She handed him the glass and he took a sip, glancing around. Everybody was looking at him, including the gunnery sergeant. Somebody put the needle back onto the record, and Tex Benecke and the Modernaires came on.

Dolly poured herself some whiskey and ginger ale. "When'd you get in town, Johnny?" she asked.

"This afternoon."

"Where you been?"

"Up to my ass in Japs."

She looked at him, saw the new scars on his face, and remembered how much she'd loved him, the toughest man she'd ever met. Sometimes she loved him and sometimes she hated him, but she'd never stopped loving his allotment, which showed up every month.

"How long you gonna be in town?" she asked.

"Seven days."

"You staying here?"

"I hadn't intended to."

"It's your house, Johnny, just like you said. You can stay here if you want to."

"I don't know if I want to."

"You should let bygones be bygones. You can't carry a grudge forever."

"Who can't?"

"Well, maybe *you* can."

"There are some things a man just can't forget."

"If he don't want to forget, I guess he won't."

"Sometimes memories don't go away whether you want them to or not."

She wrinkled her forehead and shook her head. "I don't want to talk about that. It won't lead nowheres. Come on in the kitchen, where it's quiet and we can talk in peace, okay?"

"Okay."

She turned away from him and walked toward the kitchen, and he looked at her big ass. She was really upholstered for comfort these days. She'd always been a big girl, but she'd gotten bigger. He followed her into the kitchen and looked at the old Frigidaire, the electric Donald Duck clock on the wall, the little Emerson radio that she listened to when she cooked and did the dishes.

"Have a seat, Johnny," she said. "Can I get you something to eat?"

"Yeah, I'm a little hungry," he replied, sitting in the breakfast nook. There wasn't much room in there; he'd never liked the damn breakfast nook. "What you got?"

"Would you like a chicken sandwich?"

"That sounds good."

"With a little lettuce and mayonnaise?"

"Sure."

She opened the Frigidaire door and took out the makings for a sandwich. "Well, I never thought I'd see you again," she said, taking the cover off the glass container that held the chicken meat. "When I saw you out there I couldn't believe my eyes."

"Who's the gunnie?"

She knew exactly who he was talking with, but pretended she didn't. "The who?"

"The Marine gunnery sergeant."

"Oh, that's Jack."

"You going out with him or something?"

"What if I was?"

"So you're going out with him."

"I didn't say that."

"You didn't have to."

She looked at him angrily. "Well, what am I supposed to do, wait for you to show up? I haven't seen you for two years, you son of a bitch, and I wrote you a letter six months ago, and I never got an answer."

"I never got no letter from you," he lied.

"You *didn't?*"

"No, but mail service ain't so hot up at the front." That was another lie, because the Army always was very scrupulous about mail, no matter what the circumstances.

"What front was that, Johnny?"

60

"Guadalcanal."

"I figured that's where you were. They always send old Johnny Butsko where the shit is the deepest."

He smiled faintly. "Ain't that the truth."

"Was it as bad there as the papers said it was?"

"I don't know what the papers said, but it probably was worse."

"Well, at least you're still alive and kicking."

She finished making the sandwich and put the extra stuff back into the refrigerator, then carried the chicken sandwich on white bread to him on a dish. He rolled up the sleeves of his khaki shirt as she set the plate before him and sat down on the other side of the table.

He rolled his sleeves up to his elbows, and she saw on his forearms the new scars that he'd got from hand-to-hand fighting with Japs on Guadalcanal. Without thinking about what she was doing, she reached out and laid her hand on one of the scars.

"Jesus, Johnny, the things you must've been through."

Without replying, he lifted half of the chicken sandwich and bit off most of it, chomping away, not wanting to look at her eyes because he was afraid she might hypnotize him.

"The fighting's all over on Guadalcanal," she said. "Where are you going next?"

"I don't know, but if I did I couldn't tell you." He put the rest of the half-sandwich into his mouth and sipped some whiskey.

She looked at him and knit her eyebrows together. There was something about him that she just couldn't stop loving, and she knew he loved her, but their marriage had been five years of fighting over everything. They used every trick in the book on each other, and at times he fell back on the violence that came so easily to him, while she'd done all the sneaky, shitty things that women do. The result had been a continual state of war until he'd shipped out for the Phillipines.

"Johnny," she said, "I wish we could get along."

He reached for the other half-sandwich. "We can't get along because you like to fuck around too much, Dolly."

"Everything I've done I've done because of you." She reached toward him. "Gimme a cigarette, willya?"

He took out his pack of cigarettes and tossed them in front of her. She upended the pack, caught one, and put it in her mouth. He placed his Zippo on the table and she picked it up, flicking the wheel in front of her cigarette.

He took a sip of whiskey. "What do you mean, you fucked around because of me? Why are you blaming everything on me?"

"What did you expect me to do, sit home and twiddle my thumbs while you were away?"

"No, but you don't have to fuck other guys."

"I get lonely, Johnny. I can't help it."

"That's not my fault. A lot of women don't fuck around when their husbands are away."

"A lot of women don't have any life in them."

Butsko grunted as he put the last piece of sandwich in his mouth. It was true: A lot of women were dull, and Johnny didn't consider them attractive. But he'd always been attracted to Dolly because she'd been a live wire. That's why he'd married her so. Even now she was radiating heat and light across the table.

"The only way to deal with a woman like you," Butsko said, "is to chain you to the goddamn bed. Too bad that's against the law."

"You're the only man I've ever really loved, Johnny."

"Knock it off, Dolly."

"You don't believe me?"

"How can I believe you? You lie so much."

"Let's not argue. We've been over this ground a hundred times already." She leaned forward and placed her hand on his. "We should stop talking and just go upstairs."

He grinned. "You think so?"

"Yeah."

"With all these people here?"

"To hell with them."

Butsko pushed the empty dish away and looked at her, wondering what to do. He wanted to go upstairs with her, but he was also mad at her. She'd broken his heart too many times. But she still looked good to him. Her big tits filled out in front of her dress and she had a twinkle in her eye.

She shook her head slowly. "You just can't forget, can you?"

"Guess not. A man likes to think that his wife is all his."

"I'm all yours right now."

"What about tomorrow?"

62

"Why are you worried about tomorrow? Today isn't over yet."

Butsko flashed on Guadalcanal, when the fighting was the toughest and he had thought he was going to die any moment. He'd be back in the war soon and maybe he'd run into that bullet that had his name on it. What the hell—he might as well take his pleasure where he could find it, and Dolly sure was a pleasure. He'd love to squeeze her big tits again, just like in the old days.

"Is it that hard to make up your mind?" she asked.

"Let's go," he said.

He slid out of the breakfast nook and looked down at her. She had a wise-ass smile on her face as she arose beside him.

"Lead the way," he said.

She touched her lips lightly to his, sending a thrill up his spine. Then she turned and walked out of the kitchen. They passed through the living room, where the record player was blasting and Dolly's guests were dancing and partying. Everybody noticed them, and some of the guests appeared amused, while others were perplexed.

One of them was angry. He was Jack Crane, the Marine gunnery sergeant who was Dolly's current boyfriend, or at least that's what he thought. He looked down the hall and saw Dolly opening the door to her bedroom, with Butsko standing behind her, his hand on her waist. Jack felt the temperature rise underneath his collar. She couldn't just slough him off like that, after all the presents he'd given her and all the money he'd lent her without ever expecting to get it back.

He set down his glass and walked down the hall. Butsko and Dolly heard him coming and turned around. Jack had had drunk too much and wasn't in a sensible mood. The booze had loosened his inhibitions and permitted him to get angry.

"Where the hell you going!" Jack said.

Dolly looked at him with disbelief. Had he lost his mind? At that moment she realized for the first time that Jack was a big asshole.

"Mind your own business," Dolly said. "Go back to the party."

"This is my business!" Jack replied. "You just can't walk out on me like this!"

"You're drunk. You'd better sit down someplace."

With a glance at Butsko, who was surprisingly calm at this point, she walked into the bedroom. Butsko followed her. She turned to close the door, but Jack pushed hard and it flew open again, causing Dolly to lose her balance and stumble backward. Jack stood hulking in the doorway with his wide shoulders and florid face. His light brown hair was shorn to a quarter-inch in length, and his ears were large and protruding.

"What the fuck you think this is, Dolly?" Jack demanded.

"Who the hell you think you're talking to?" she replied.

He pointed at her. "I'm talking to you! You can't just throw me away like an old shoe!"

"Get lost, Jack," she said. "You're making a nuisance of yourself."

"Whataya mean, 'Get lost'!" He stormed into the bedroom, balling up his fists. "You've cost me a fortune, you fucking cunt! You can't treat me this way!"

"Hey," Butsko said softly, "that's my wife you're talking to. I think you'd better calm down."

Jack looked at Butsko and sneered. "Your wife? Don't make me laugh! She's screwed just about every soldier, sailor, and Marine who's ever been to Honolulu! Your wife? She's the town pump, for Chrissakes!"

Butsko's movements were surprisingly swift for such a big man. At one moment Butsko was standing a few feet away from Jack, and in the next moment Butsko was charging like a wild bull. Butsko dived on Jack, grabbed him by his shirt, and threw him against the wall. There was a tremendous crashing sound and the dresser shook, Dolly's perfume bottles toppling over. Jack bounced off the wall and came back at Butsko, swinging.

Butsko blocked the first punch and hammered Jack in the gut, while Jack punched Butsko in the mouth. Butsko hooked up to Jack's head, and Jack threw a punch that Butsko caught on his shoulder, but Butsko's hook was more powerful, staggering Jack. Butsko slammed Jack in the mouth, splitting his lip open, and Jack reached deep inside himself for a killer punch that landed squarely on Butsko's nose, busting it up.

The pain and blood drove Butsko wild. He ran toward Jack, drew back his arm, and threw an incredible blow. It hit Jack on the chin and lifted him off his feet, sending him flying into the hallway. In another part of the house women screamed and men came running.

Jack lay on his back in the hallway, trying to get up, and Butsko jumped on top of him, straddling him and punching him in the mouth until another Marine sergeant dived onto Butsko. Behind him came yet another Marine sergeant, who also piled on.

Butsko fell onto his back under the weight of the two Marine sergeants, who tried to pin down his hands and punch his lights out at the same time. Butsko, in his rage and pain, thought it was just like those hand-to-hand battles with the Japs on Guadalcanal. With a mighty roar he swung around and broke loose, delivering a backhand punch to one of the Marines, and then heaved hard with his belly, pushing the other Marine to the side.

Butsko snarled and jumped to his feet. One of the Marine sergeants was on his knees, and Butsko kicked him in the teeth, then darted in the direction of the other Marine, who was on his feet, raising his arms to protect himself. Butsko punched toward his face, but the Marine's fists were raised to protect himself and he blocked the blow, although its force shook him up. The Marine swung down with a hook to Butsko's kidney and landed on target, but Butsko was too angry to feel pain. He grabbed the Marine by the throat and squeezed hard, and the Marine clawed at Butsko's hands, drawing blood, but Butsko didn't let go.

"Stop it!" Dolly screamed. "You'll kill him!"

Butsko heard her and came back to his senses. He loosened his grip and let the Marine, whose face was blue, drop to the floor.

A crowd of women and servicemen were in the hallway, and one of the women screamed: "You killed him!"

Butsko turned to face her and she jumped on him like a wildcat, trying to scratch out his eyes. She succeeded in digging red lines across his face, and then Dolly shrieked and grabbed her by her long hair, pulling her backward. Another woman in the hallway jumped on Dolly, and then another woman, who was a friend of Dolly's, jumped on that woman.

Meanwhile Jack had picked himself up off the floor and was reaching into his pocket for his jackknife.

"Watch out!" somebody yelled.

Butsko turned around and saw Jack pull the jackknife out of his pocket, but before Jack could open the blade, Butsko grabbed Jack's wrist with one hand and belted him in the mouth. Then another Marine jumped Butsko from behind and Butsko threw him over his shoulder into the crowd in the corridor. Women yelped and men got out of the way as Butsko went after him. The Marine got up and ran away toward the living room, and Butsko followed, tackling him from behind. Both of them went crashing into the table that held all the booze, and it tipped over, bottles and glasses flying everywhere.

The first Marine followed Butsko into the living room, saw him tussling with one of his buddies on the floor, and picked a lamp off an end table, raising it up in the air behind Butsko. He smashed the lamp against Butsko's head and Butsko fell to the floor, unconscious.

"I got him!" the first Marine shouted.

Jack came staggering into the room. *"Where is he?"* He looked down and saw Butsko lying on his stomach. Jack took out his jackknife and opened the blade. Women screamed and Jack held the knife in his fist with the blade pointing downward. He raised the knife in the air and was about to plunge it into Butsko's back, when Butsko came to.

"Look out!" somebody yelled.

Butsko rolled over suddenly as the knife came down, and it stabbed into the floor. Butsko bounded to his feet, saw a whiskey bottle lying intact on the floor, picked it up by the neck, and smashed the bottle against the wall.

Jack pulled his jackknife out of the floor and turned to face Butsko, who advanced with the broken whiskey bottle in his hand.

"You're a dead man," Butsko said.

"We'll see about that!" Jack replied, getting into a knife-fighter's crouch.

At that moment Dolly burst into the room, her dress torn and her hair all messed up. She took one look at the both of them and her eyes widened.

"Stop that!" she yelled.

"Stand back," Butsko replied.

Dolly leaped forward and got between the two of them, holding up both her hands. "I don't care if you beat each other

66

to death, but no knives and no broken bottles!"

Both men hesitated, because to get at one another they'd have to go through Dolly.

"Well," said Jack, "I ain't dropping my knife unless he drops that there broken bottle."

"I ain't dropping this bottle unless he drops that knife," Butsko said.

Dolly was getting furious. "You're both like a couple of goddamned kids! I said drop those things, both of you!"

Butsko didn't want to do it, but he thought he should take the chance. He was liable to kill Jack, and that would have very serious consequences. "Okay," he said, and he let the broken bottle fall to the floor, where it shattered.

Dolly looked at Jack, "It's your turn now."

With a victorious shout, Jack pushed Dolly out of the way and charged Butsko, driving his knife toward Butsko's heart. Butsko dodged to the side and grabbed Jack's wrist with both his hands. He kneed Jack in the balls, elbowed him in the eye, and slammed Jack's wrist against the wall. The knife fell out of Jack's hand and Butsko picked Jack up, raised him over his head, and threw him at the plate glass window in the living room. Jack crashed through the window, landing with shards of glass on the front lawn.

Butsko ran out the door and stomped on Jack's head twice before another Marine jumped on his back. Butsko grabbed his arm, bent down, and threw him over his shoulder, then dived on top of him, punching him in the face.

The crowd in the house poured outside. Dolly led them, grabbing Butsko's collar, trying to pull him off the Marine. "Stop it!" she yelled. "You'll kill him!"

The Marine was unconscious and his face a bloody mess. Butsko got to his feet and let Dolly pull him backward. He glanced at Jack lying still on the ground, his face all fucked up, and then, for the first time, he heard the police sirens.

SIX . . .

The room was shabby and filled with smoke, and an electric light inside a green lampshade hung over the round table, where the men played stud poker. There were soldiers, sailors, and Marines, Hawaiians and Chinese, and even a fighter pilot stationed at Hickam Field, watching the dealer flicking the cards off the top of the deck.

"Possible straight forming there," said the dealer, throwing out the cards. "There's a pair of queens showing . . . possible flush forming. . . ."

The dealer's voice droned on, and Frankie La Barbara looked at his cards. He had a pair of sixes showing and one in the hole—not the best hand in the world—and the guy with the pair of queens might have something in the hole, too, otherwise he wouldn't be betting the way he was. Or was he bluffing? Frankie was willing to pay to find out. He had five hundred dollars in chips stacked in front of him and thought the others ought to have a chance to win some back of the money they'd lost. He'd announced a half hour ago that he was leaving at midnight, and midnight was only a few minutes away. This would be Frankie's last hand.

The cards kept coming around and the bets increased. Some of the gamblers dropped out, and when it was down and dirty, Frankie was in the game with the guy who had the queens showing and two other guys, the first with a pair of jacks showing and the other with the possible flush. Frankie drew an ace; he already had another ace in the hole, so now he had a full house with three sixes and the two aces.

The white chips were one dollar, the red chips two dollars, and the blue chips five dollars. The guy with the queens showing was a Torpedoman's Mate Second Class, wearing his white swabby uniform with his white cap on the back of his head; he was the one who'd opened. He picked up one of the blue chips and threw it onto the pot, looking at the guy to his left, the fighter pilot from Hickam Field, who had the possible flush. The pilot was a tall, skinny guy with a big hooked nose, who looked something like a young Jimmy Durante, and he peeked at his cards in the hole, puffing the cigarette dangling from the corner of his mouth. Then he threw a blue chip onto the pile.

"I'm still in," he said.

Everybody looked at the corporal with the Signal Corps insignia on his collar, who had the pair of jacks showing.

"You in?" asked the sailor.

"Yeah." He tossed out a blue chip.

Next was Frankie La Barbara, whose cunt cap was high on the back of his head and low over his forehead. His shirt was unbuttoned and his tie loosened, and although he'd shaved that morning, he needed to shave again.

"Whataya say, big boy?" asked the sailor.

Frankie was tired and hung over from all the booze he'd been drinking. He'd been sitting in the same spot for four hours and he just wanted to get the hell out of there with his winnings, but he was a gambling man and couldn't back away from the challenge. *I wonder what that motherfucker has got*, he said to himself.

"Okay," Frankie said, digging into his pile of chips, "here's one to stay in"—he threw a blue chip on the pot—"and I'll bump you two." He threw out two more blue chips.

"He's bluffing," said somebody standing behind the sailor.

"There's only one way to find that out," Frankie replied, taking his pack of cigarettes from his shirt pocket.

"Shit," said the corporal with the two jacks. "I'm out."

Frankie looked at the sailor. "Shit or get off the pot."

"I'm staying. Two, and here's four more."

"Jesus," said the fighter pilot. "You two guys are really going at it. Well, I'll stay in. It's only money."

He threw his chips onto the pile, and everybody looked at Frankie La Barbara. Under normal circumstances Frankie would have dropped out at that point. Three sixes and two aces weren't a very strong hand, but it was his last hand and he wanted to let somebody win some money back, so there wouldn't be any hard feelings. Besides, something told him the sailor was bluffing. The sailor looked like the kind of guy who was full of shit.

"Here's my four," Frankie said, "and here's five more."

The little back room became silent. Frankie had just raised the betting by $25, exactly half a private's monthly pay. A corporal only earned $66 per month, and the fighter pilot, the best-paid man at the table, earned $166 per month, but he had to pay for his uniforms and meals out of that.

"Let's go, girls," Frankie said, blowing smoke into the air. "I ain't got all night."

"I'm in," said the sailor, counting out five blue chips and tossing them onto the pot.

"I must be crazy," said the fighter pilot, "but I'll see what you got."

He threw the five blue chips onto the pile. The pot was now worth nearly two hundred dollars and was the biggest pot of the night.

Frankie turned up his cards. "Three sixes and two aces," he said.

"Shit!" said the sailor, pounding his fist on the table. He turned over his cards in the hole: All he had was the pair of queens and a pair of jacks.

"I knew you were bluffing," Frankie said with a grin.

The sailor gave him a dirty look. Everybody looked at the fighter pilot.

"What you got?" asked Frankie.

"Read 'em and weep," said the fighter pilot, turning over his cards.

He'd made his flush, and it wasn't just a plain flush: It was a straight flush. The fighter pilot leaned over and wrapped his arms around the pot, pulling it toward him.

"Never bluff a bluffer," he said.

Frankie stood up. "I'm leaving," he said.

"Where you going?" asked the sailor.

"What's it to you?"

"Hey," the sailor said, looking at Frankie's chips, "you oughtta give us a chance to win some of that back."

"I told you a half hour ago that I was leaving at midnight, and it's midnight. You had your chance. If you can't stand to lose, you shouldn't gamble."

"I shouldn't gamble with cheaters," the sailor said. "That's what I shouldn't do."

Frankie froze, his hand on his pile of chips. "Who're you calling a cheater?"

"If the shoe fits, wear it."

"Hey, swab-jockey," Frankie said, "don't piss me off."

The sailor stood up and hitched his fingers in his belt. "You won too many hands, dogface. I smell a fish."

"You smell your mother's pussy," Frankie snarled.

The sailor stitched his eyebrows together. "Say that again."

"You smell your mother's pussy, and you look like it too."

The sailor reached into his pocket and came out with a switchblade. He hit the button and it opened up. "I think somebody needs to teach you a lesson, dogface."

Frankie raised his knee in a sudden lightning movement and pulled his bayonet out of the scabbard tied to his leg.

The old Chinese guy in a white suit stepped out of the shadows, and he had a big Army-issue .45 in his hands. "Put those knives away," he said in his high-pitched, reedy voice.

Two other Chinese guys joined him, also with guns in their hands.

"You heard him," one said.

The fighter pilot stood up, conscious of his responsibilities as an officer and a gentleman. "C'mon guys," he said, "let's not start any shit."

"He started it," Frankie said, "and I'm gonna finish it."

The old Chinese guy shook his head. "Not in here you ain't. You want to fight, you go outside."

Frankie shrugged. "That's okay by me."

"Me too," said the sailor.

"Oh, no you don't," the fighter pilot said. "If you guys fight each other outside, I'm calling the fucking MPs." He looked at the sailor. "And I'm gonna tell them who the first one was who pulled a knife."

The sailor turned toward the fighter pilot, pointing his knife at him. "I can take care of you too."

A blackjack came down behind the sailor and hit him squarely on top of his head. His eyes rolled back and his legs gave out. He crashed toward the floor; behind him was another Chinese guy, with a blackjack in his hand.

The old Chinese guy bent over and picked up the switchblade knife from the floor, folding the blade and dropping in inside his pocket.

"Get rid of him," he said.

Other Chinese men picked up the sailor and carried him out the back door. Frankie inserted his bayonet into its scabbard and hoped they'd dump the bastard into the bay.

"You," the old Chinese man said to Frankie, "get out of here and don't come back."

"How come?" Frankie asked, his feelings hurt. "I didn't start it."

"We don't like crazy guys with knives in here. Cash in your chips and get out."

"I been thrown out of better places," Frankie said, scooping up his chips.

He carried them to the cashier, an elderly Chinese woman who was evidently the old guy's wife. She gave Frankie the money in twenties and tens, which made a big fat roll. He stuffed it into his pocket and headed for the back door.

"So long, everybody," he said.

A Chinese man opened the door and Frankie stepped out into the back alley. It was dark and gloomy and he couldn't see the tough guys who'd carried away the sailor. Whistling a tune, Frankie thrust his hands in his pockets and walked down the alley to the street, which glowed in the light of street lamps and neon. He was tired but happy and thought he'd check into a fancy hotel for a good night of sleep.

He reached the street and turned left, heading for the center of the city, where the fancy hotels were. Drunken servicemen careened all around him, and barkers invited him into the girlie bars. Raucous music assailed him from all directions. He was glad he had his bayonet with him, because you never knew who might be waiting in an alley to beat up a soldier and take his money.

He came to a corner and looked both ways. His eyes fastened on a neon sign that said CURTIS HOTEL.

"Curtis Hotel," Frankie muttered. "Where have I heard that before?"

Then it hit him. The Curtis Hotel was the classy whorehouse where Butsko had told Bannon to go. Suddenly Frankie didn't feel so tired anymore. He thought he'd take a walk over there and see what the whores looked like. His pocket held over five hundred dollars and he felt like a millionaire.

Frankie headed for the hotel, straightening his necktie and taking off his cunt cap to smooth down his wavy hair. He put his cunt cap back on and tucked in his shirt so he'd look neat. The women in the Curtis were only whores, but Frankie always liked to look his best for the opposite sex. He approached the door of the hotel, threw the butt of his cigarette into the gutter, and opened the door; he didn't even pause to think about it. Climbing the stairs, he came to the second floor corridor, with its crystal chandeliers and red wallpaper.

Not bad at all, Frankie thought, strolling to the desk. The old madam sat behind it with two mean-looking Hawaiian guys. "Hi, there," said Frankie, leaning over the counter. "Where are the girls?"

The old madam smiled. "Upstairs, soldier. What's your name?"

"What you wanna know my name for?"

The old madam put her hand on the telephone. "So's I can tell them to expect you upstairs."

"Just call me Frankie."

"You're not carrying any weapons with you, are you, Frankie?"

"Naw," said Frankie, an innocent smile on his face. "I come here to get laid, not to fight with people."

"That's good, because we don't want any trouble here."

"Then I musta come to the right place, because I don't want any trouble either."

Frankie headed for the staircase and climbed up to the second floor. *They seem awfully jumpy at the front desk,* he thought.

Maybe they had some problems here tonight. Mae stood at the top of the stairs, looking at him suspiciously.

"You Frankie?" she asked.

"Sure am."

"Right this way."

She looked him up and down, and Frankie was starting to get spooked. "What's going on here?" he asked.

"What do you mean?" asked Mae.

"Everybody's looking at me like I'm a cop."

She smiled and took off his cunt cap, running her fingers through his hair. "I know you're not a cop," she said. "You're just a soldier boy with a hard-on, right?"

"You got it, baby, but why's everybody so nervous?"

"Well, we had a little trouble here tonight, but it's all over now."

"What happened?"

"Somebody got drunk and went crazy." She opened the door to a room off the corridor, and it was full of girls in cocktail dresses. "Have a seat in there. Can I get you a drink?"

"Whiskey and ginger ale."

Mae left and Frankie entered the room. One sailor sat in the corner, surrounded by girls, and a GI was in another corner, likewise occupied. Frankie looked around for the prettiest girl he could find and sat down next to her.

"Hey, baby," he said, "what's your name?"

"Trixie," she replied. She was a redhead with green eyes.

"Hey, I bet they call you Trixie because you do funny tricks."

"You bet your ass I do," she said with a wink.

"I wouldn't bet my ass, baby. It's the only ass I got and I might need it for something someday."

The girl sitting on the other side of Frankie was Julie, and she looked at the patch on Frankie's shoulder. "Hey, this guy is in the same outfit as the guy who went nuts tonight!"

"No kidding!" said Trixie.

"Look and see for yourself," Julie said.

"I didn't see the other guy, so I don't know what his patch looked like."

Frankie stared at Julie, thinking that very few men from the Eighty-first Division could be in Honolulu, since the Eighty-first was stationed on Guadalcanal and furloughs were hard to get, even for officers. "You mean a guy wearing a patch like this went nuts in here tonight?"

"That's right," she replied.

"Did you see him?"

"I sure did. I was talking with him just like I'm talking to you."

"What he look like?"

"You think you might know him?"

"You never know."

"I hope you're not like him, because he was really crazy."

"What he look like?"

"Well," said Julie, "he was about as tall as you, but he was built slim and he had light-brown hair. He wasn't bad-looking at all, and he wore one of them combat pins on his shirt, just like you."

Frankie was jolted by the thought that the description fit Bannon, who had been on his way here earlier. "Did you get his name?"

"I forgot it," Julie said.

"How about you?" Frankie asked Trixie.

"I don't know. But Nettie knows."

"Who's Nettie?"

"She's the girl he was with when he went nuts."

"Where's she now?"

"Probably with a customer. She'll be back in a little while."

"What she look like?"

"She's real small and kinda cute, if you like runts."

Frankie grinned and pulled out his pack of cigarettes. He lit a cigarette and dropped his Zippo into his pant pocket. The door opened and Mae walked in with Frankie's drink.

"Anybody else want anything?" Mae asked.

The sailor ordered a beer and the GI asked for whiskey. Mae left to get the drinks. The phone rang out in the hall. Trixie turned to Frankie.

"Are you here to drink or are you here to fuck?"

"Both," Frankie said. "I haven't been laid in almost a year."

"You're probably pretty rusty."

"I doubt it."

"You don't seem in any hurry to get laid."

"I'm tired," Frankie said. "I didn't get much sleep last night

76

and I'm just coming out of a four-hour poker game."

"Win any money?"

"You'd better believe it."

"How much?"

"Enough to buy your little ass for a couple of weeks."

"Yeah?"

"Yeah."

She winked. "Let's go to my room."

"After I finish my drink."

"You can finish it in my room."

The door opened and two sailors from Pearl Harbor stumbled in, drunk out of their minds, their white caps askew on their heads. Trixie and Julie looked at the sailors and saw two live ones.

"Listen, honey," Trixie said to Frankie, "if you're not ready yet, I'll see you later."

"Sure thing, doll."

Julie was already on her feet, slinking across the floor, placing her arm around the shoulders of one of the sailors, who leaned from side to side and blinked his eyes. Trixie came at the other sailor from the side, bending over and sticking her tongue into his ear, making him roll his eyes and shiver.

Frankie watched with amusement as the two whores vamped the sailors and led them out of the room before the sailors even had a chance to sit down. It reminded him of the whores in a joint one of his uncles owned up in Harlem. Frankie had lost his cherry to one of the whores there when he was only fourteen years old, and he'd spent a lot of time in the place subsequently, because his uncle didn't make him pay.

The door opened again and a tiny little woman with long brown hair entered, wearing a blue silk dress. Frankie realized she must be Nettie, the little one Julie had told him about, the one Bannon had gone with. He stood and walked toward her, carrying his drink and cigarette in his left hand, smiling in a friendly, sexy way.

"What's your name, sweetheart?" he asked.

"Nettie."

"Where's your room, you pretty little thing?"

Nettie smiled back, because she loved compliments. "Just follow me."

Frankie heard the sound of the Old South in her voice and

loved her big brown eyes. He could see why Bannon had selected her. She was an excellent choice, even though her nose was a little too small and pointed up too much. She led him down the hall and opened the door to her room.

"Well, what can I do for you?" she asked when they were inside.

Frankie looked down at her. "What do you recommend?"

"The half-and-half for seven-fifty."

"It's a deal," Frankie said. He took out his roll of money and Nettie's big eyes became bigger. He threw her a ten-dollar bill. "Keep the change, honey."

"I'll be right back," she replied. "You can take your clothes off."

She left the room with the money, but Frankie didn't take his clothes off. He wasn't horny, because he was worried that the guy who'd gone crazy earlier might be Bannon, who was his closest buddy in the Army. Frankie stood in front of the mirror and looked at himself as he sipped his drink. His neat, pressed uniform had become rumpled, and his eyes were at half-mast. The Guadalcanal sun had made his skin very dark, and that caused the white of his eyes to glow as if lights were behind them. He hoped Bannon wasn't the guy who went crazy.

Nettie returned to the room and saw him looking at himself in front of the mirror. "Hey, how come you're not taking your clothes off? Do you like to do it with your clothes on?"

"Don't rush me, honey."

"For seven-fifty you don't get to stay here all night."

Frankie took out his fat roll of bills and showed it to her. "I'll pay whatever I have to. Relax. Have a seat."

Nettie sat nervously on the edge of the bed. "Can't you get it up?" she asked. "If you can't, I know what to do."

"I can get it up. Don't worry." Frankie sat in the chair and sipped his drink. "I heard you had a little trouble here tonight."

She stiffened. "Where'd you hear that?"

"Everybody's talking about it. Do you remember the guy's name?"

"What guy?"

"The guy who went nuts."

She nodded. "Yeah, I remember his name. Are you an MP."

Frankie shook his head. "Nope. I just think I might know the guy."

She jumped off the bed and ran for the door. He lunged for her and grabbed her wrist.

"Let me go!" she said.

"What's the matter with you?"

"I don't want any trouble!"

"There ain't gonna be any trouble," Frankie said in a low, soothing voice.

"It ain't my fault!"

"Nobody said it was your fault. Relax and tell me the guy's name. I'm not gonna hurt you. If it's my buddy, I'll have to find out where he is, and if it isn't, we'll just fuck on the bed."

There was something about Frankie that scared the shit out of her, but he didn't seem angry; he was only concerned about his buddy. Also, she didn't want to call the bouncers again, because the boss might decide she was a troublemaker and fire her.

"What was his name?" Frankie asked.

"Bannon," she replied.

Frankie closed his eyes. "Oh, God."

"You know him?"

"He's my best buddy in the Army."

Nettie got scared again. "It wasn't my fault!"

"Relax," Frankie said. He let her go and stumbled back to the chair, dropping into it. He sipped his drink and looked up at her. "What happened?"

She crossed her arms and walked toward him, swinging her hips from side to side. "Everything was going all right until we were finished and he was getting dressed. I really kind of liked him, because, you know, he's nice-looking and polite and all. Well, then, all of a sudden he started talking crazy. He said he wanted me to leave with him and get married. When I said no, he picked me up and started to carry me away. I screamed for help and the bouncers came. There was a fight and your friend killed one of the bouncers. Then the cops came and arrested your friend." Nettie covered her face with with her hands and sat on the bed. "It was awful. Everything always happens to me."

"Jesus," Frankie said. "He killed a guy?"

"Yes?"

"How?"

"With a knife. A switchblade."

"You're sure the guy was dead."

"That's what the police doctor said, and the other bouncer is in the hospital. Your friend beat the shit out of him."

Frankie went slack on the chair. If Bannon had killed somebody, he was in big trouble. It was manslaughter from the sound of it and Bannon could get put away for a long time unless it could be proved that he had fought in self-defense. Frankie knew something about the law because all his uncles were in the Mob back in New York City and he'd worked for them, doing odd jobs like shaking people down and providing muscle when muscle was needed.

"Who was the first one to pull a knife?" Frankie said.

"Your friend."

"You sure?"

Nettie thought for a few moments. "No, it was Carl."

"Carl was one of the bouncers?"

"Yes."

"You sure?"

"Yes."

"Anybody else see Carl pull the knife first?"

"Lots of people."

"And the Honolulu police took my friend away?"

"Yes."

"When'd all this happen?"

"Around seven-thirty."

Frankie took out another cigarette and lit it up. *That fucking crazy cowboy Bannon. The bouncers must have crowded him a little and he thought he was back on Guadalcanal. I've got to spring him,* Frankie thought. *He's my buddy and I've got to get him out of there.*

Nettie cried softly as she remembered the whole ordeal. "It was awful," she said, "the worst thing that ever happened to me in my life."

"You're an asshole," Frankie said. "You should've gone with him."

She lowered her knuckles from her tear-stained face. "He wouldn't have married me!"

"Oh, yes he would've. If he said he'd do it, he'd do it. I've known him for nearly two years, and I've never seen him go back on his word. When he said something, you could build a house on it." Frankie's face took on a disgusted expression.

"He must've fell in love with you, you stupid bitch, and he wanted to get you out of your crummy fucking life. I don't know what he saw in you, but he saw something, and thanks to you he's in jail right now."

Nettie stared at him for a few moments and then cried uncontrollably. She covered her face with her hands and collapsed sideways onto the bed, her body wracked with sobs. Ever since the cops took Bannon away, she had been distressed by what had happened, and now she was breaking down completely.

Frankie looked at her and felt no pity. Bannon was the one he was worried about. He pulled his bayonet out of its scabbard and walked towards her. Grabbing her hair in his hand, he pushed her onto her back and laid the blade against her throat.

"I ought to fucking kill you for what you did," Frankie said through clenched teeth. "But you're just a dumb fucking whore and you're not worth the trouble."

Frankie pulled the bayonet back and pressed it into the scabbard attached to his leg. He gulped down the remainder of his whiskey, put on his cunt cap, and reached into his pocket, taking out his roll of bills, peeling off a ten. He threw the ten onto the bed beside Nettie, who stared at him, horrified and trembling, and then he walked out of the room, slamming the door behind him.

Nettie looked at the ten-dollar bill, thought for a few moments, and then rolled over onto her stomach, covering her face with her hands and crying pathetically.

SEVEN . . .

Frankie pushed open the front door of the Curtis Hotel and stepped onto the sidewalk which pulsated with the flashing of neon lights. Drunken servicemen still stumbled around, and all the bars were open, although business was slow that time of the month. He looked at his watch: It was one o'clock in the morning. *What the hell should I do now?* he thought.

He walked toward the center of town, his hands in his pockets, and tried to work out a plan of action. He'd have to find out what jail Bannon had been taken to and go to see him. Maybe he could hire a lawyer and spring him in the morning, but what would the Army do? Maybe the Army had jurisdiction. Frankie didn't know all the ins and outs of the Army's legal system, but he knew who would have that information: Butsko. Frankie realized that the best thing to do was find Butsko and tell him what had happened. Butsko would know what to do. Butsko *always* knew what to do.

Frankie took his notepad out of his shirt pocket. Before he and the others had parted earlier in the day, Bustko had given them an address where he could be reached if anybody needed him, and Frankie had written down the address. He found it in the book and then looked around for a cab.

None were visible, but he figured he'd run into one before long. He headed for the center of Honolulu, walked swiftly, wide awake now. He wondered if Bannon had been hurt in the fight and cursed himself for not asking the whore. Actually the whore wasn't bad-looking at all, but Frankie didn't want to tell her so and give her the satisfaction. He could understand why Bannon had fallen for her. She was like a little bird in paradise, but she had no common sense. If Bannon had married her, he would have taken care of her for the rest of his life.

He came to a street lined with bars. He wanted to go into one of them for a drink, but he told himself he didn't have time. The sooner he saw Butsko, the sooner they could get Bannon out of the clink. Butsko would take care of everything. Butsko was the man you could always rely on in a pinch.

A few blocks later Frankie saw a taxicab pulling up to the curb of an apartment building. He ran toward the taxicab as the rear door opened and two long beautiful legs swung out toward the sidewalk. A tall blonde followed the legs out and stood up. She heard Frankie approaching and spun around.

"Hey, baby," Frankie said to her, "what's going on?"

She looked at him like he was a piece of shit, and then a major with a black mustache got out of the cab.

"Something wrong, soldier?" the major asked.

"No, sir. Uh-uh."

The major looked at him disdainfully and Frankie wanted to deck him. There was no one around and he could get away in the cab, but maybe he couldn't get away, and one man from the recon platoon in the can was enough.

The blonde hooked her arm in the major's and walked with him to the front door of the apartment building. Frankie dropped into the backseat of the cab and closed the door.

"Where to?" asked the driver, a tubby Hawaiian guy.

"Twenty-nine—ten Palmetto Drive," Bannon replied, reading from his notebook.

The driver shifted into gear and drove off. Frankie took out a cigarette and lit it up, watching the bars and hotels pass by his window. He was thinking about the sexy blonde and realized that he could probably be with somebody like her right now, and she could be copping his joint, but instead he had to do something for Bannon.

"Dumb fucking cowboy," he muttered.

"What was that?" asked the driver.

"I wasn't talking to you," Frankie said. "Step on the gas, will you? I'm in a hurry."

"Sure thing," the driver said.

Forty-five minutes later the cab stopped in front of 2910 Palmetto Drive. A light was on in one of the rooms, Frankie thought Butsko was probably fucking his old lady, and the last person he wanted to see was Frankie La Barbara. All the lights in the other houses was out, and the street was lit only by streetlamps. Frankie paid the driver, gave him a big tip, and got out of the cab. He straightened out his shirt and tucked it in neatly, because he was afraid to be sloppy in front of Butsko, who would kick his ass if he looked sloppy.

He repositioned his cunt cap on his head and walked to the front door of the house, noticing that the living-room window was boarded up. *What the hell happened there?* Frankie wondered. *Well, I imagine Butsko will fix that window now that he's home.*

He came to the front door and knocked three times. There was no answer. He knocked again, louder this time. He figured Butsko was really going to be pissed off at him, but he'd calm down once he realized that Bannon was in trouble. Bannon had been Butsko's fair-haired boy ever since Bannon had saved Butsko's life in the fighting around Tassafaronga Point. Nobody was coming to answer the doorbell, so Frankie knocked with all his might. The door shook on its hinges.

A light came on in another part of the house, and then a light was turned on in the living room. Frankie heard footsteps approaching but they were shuffling footsteps, not firm, decisive ones like Butsko would make. He heard the inside latches being flicked, and then the door was opened by a frowzy-looking woman with big tits and a black eye.

Dolly looked at Frankie. "What the hell do you want?" she said.

"Sergeant Butsko here?" he asked.

Dolly knitted her eyebrows together, and Frankie wondered if Butsko was the one who'd punched her out. "Who are you?" she asked.

"I'm Private Frankie La Barbara, ma'am. The sergeant ever mention me to you?"

She shook her head. "No."

"Well, me and a couple of other guys from Sergeant Butsko's platoon on Guadalcanal came to Hawaii with him, and he told us to get in touch with him if any of us had any trouble, and—well, ma'am, one of us is in a lot of trouble."

"Jesus," Dolly said. "What did *he* do?"

"He killed somebody in a fight."

"Good God," she said, raising her hand to her forehead. "I think you'd better come in, Private—what you say your name was?"

"Just call me Frankie."

Frankie followed her into the living room, which Dolly had cleaned up after Butsko had been taken away, and then they entered the kitchen.

"I've just made some coffee," she said. "Have a seat."

"Is Sergeant Butsko sleeping?"

"I don't know what he's doing. The son of a bitch is in jail."

Frankie's jaw dropped open. *"Jail!"*

"That's right."

"What he do?"

"He got in a fight here. How do you think the front window got broke?"

Frankie dropped onto a bench in the breakfast nook, and Dolly lit the fire under the coffee pot.

"Who started it?"

"Johnny threw a punch at a guy who insulted me."

"He hurt him bad?"

"Damn near killed him and a couple of other guys too. There was a big brawl here. I'm lucky they didn't put me in jail."

"Jesus," Frankie said.

"Johnny is a mean son of a bitch. As soon as I saw him walk through the door I knew there was going to be trouble."

Frankie shook his head as he took out a pack of cigarettes. He realized that he'd be in jail, too, if that old Chinese guy didn't break up the beef he was having with the sailor at the card game. For all he knew, Longtree was in jail with Butsko and Bannon.

"Guadalcanal messed up our minds," Frankie said. "That's why we're all a little crazy."

"Johnny was crazy long before he ever went to Guadalcanal," Dolly said, turning off the fire under the coffee pot. She poured into two cups. "Cream and sugar?"

"Please."

She fixed Frankie's cup and carried her black coffee to the breakfast nook, sitting down opposite Frankie.

"So you're one of Johnny's boys," Dolly said. "I never met one of Johnny's boys before. He always kept me away from them. What's it like to have him for a sergeant?"

"To tell you the truth," Frankie replied, "he's kinda hard on all of us, but he knows what he's doing, so we put up with him. He's a helluva soldier."

"Yes, I imagine he would be. He loves the Army."

Frankie turned down the corners of his mouth. "I don't think he loves the Army so much."

"Yes he does. He wouldn't know what to do if he wasn't in the Army. He's one of those guys who found a home in the Army. That's why he's a lousy husband. Thank God he hasn't been shot up yet."

Frankie hesitated to tell her, but thought he ought to. "He's been shot up," he said. "You didn't know?"

"What happened?"

"He was shot in the stomach. He spent about a month in the hospital on New Caledonia. I was there too. I had malaria."

"My God," Dolly said. "I wonder if he's all better now."

"Sure he is, Mrs. Butsko. He's strong as a bull."

She smiled. "It's funny, but almost nobody calls me Mrs. Butsko. I think I like it."

Frankie sipped his coffee. "Listen," he said, "I want to try and spring the sergeant out of jail. You know what jail he's in?"

"The main Honolulu jail downtown—I think it's on Prince Street."

"I wanna go see him right away. Maybe he knows of a lawyer who can help." Frankie patted his pocket. "I won five hundred dollars playing poker tonight. I can afford the best lawyer in Honolulu for the arraignment."

She smiled. "And you'd spend it all for Johnny, wouldn't you?"

"You're damn straight."

"Yes, I know. He's that kind of guy. But you can't see him

87

now. You won't be able to see him until morning. I'll drive you into town—I got a car. We'll both see him. You can spend the night here."

"Okay," Frankie said. "If I can't see him tonight, I might as well stay here, but I want to see him first thing in the morning."

"So do I," replied Dolly.

"Where should I sleep?"

Dolly looked him over. "Anywhere you want."

He grinned. "Anywhere?"

"That's right."

Jesus, Frankie thought, *is this old broad making eyes at me?* He wouldn't mind giving her a tumble, because she was a pretty good-looking old broad, and those tits of hers were gigantic, but Butsko would wring his neck if he found out.

"Maybe I'd better sleep on the sofa," Frankie said.

"Maybe you're right," Dolly replied. "I think I've had enough excitement around here for one day."

It was three-thirty in the morning and Longtree looked up at the neon light that said CURTIS HOTEL. He glanced around and saw a few groups of soldiers and sailors lurching about, and a Marine passed out on the sidewalk. Facing the door, he felt strange about going into the whorehouse alone, because he knew that a lot of white Americans didn't like Indians. He didn't want any trouble, and if he was smart, he'd go back to his hotel room; but he'd awakened an hour ago feeling horny as a billy goat, and he remembered Butsko telling Bannon about the Curtis Hotel, which turned out to be located only a few blocks from the hotel where Longtree was staying.

Longtree looked to his right and left again and thought, *What the hell*? If there was any trouble, he'd just turn around and walk out. He wouldn't get into any arguments or punch anybody in the mouth. Butsko said they had nice clean girls in the Curtis and it was worth a try.

He opened the doors and climbed the stairs, entered a plush corridor, and approached the desk. The old madam looked at the patch on his shoulder and her gray hairs nearly stood on end.

"What can I do for you?" she asked.

"I only want a girl," Longtree said meekly, because he knew that was how white Americans wanted him to act.

"A lot of men from your division in town this week?" she asked.

"I dunno," Longtree said. He wondered what made her think that, but decided to keep his mouth shut.

"What's your name?"

"Sam Longtree."

"You an Indian?"

"Yes, ma'am, but I'm not looking for any trouble. I'll leave right now if you want me to."

"Your money's as good as anybody else's. Go on upstairs and have yourself a good time."

"Yes, ma'am. Thank you, ma'am."

Longtree moved out smartly before she could change her mind. He leaped up the stairs three at a time and saw Mae at the top, looking down.

"Boy, you sure must be horny," she said.

"Yes, ma'am."

"Well, we're real slow this time of the night. You'll have your pick of the girls."

"Yes, ma'am."

"Have a seat in this room and I'll round them up for you."

"There's no rush, ma'am. You just take your time."

"Can I get you anything to drink."

"I don't drink," Longtree lied, because he knew white Americans thought all Indians went crazy when they drank alcohol.

"I never heard of a soldier who doesn't drink," Mae said. "You sure you don't want something?"

"No, ma'am."

Mae chuckled as she walked away. Longtree entered the room, which was empty. He sat on one of the chairs and felt uncomfortable, because he was all alone. He wished Bannon or Frankie La Barbara were there with him. He was so used to being with the men from the recon platoon that it was strange to be alone.

The door opened and the whores filed in. They had thought no more customers would arrive and had been goofing off in their rooms when Mae called for them.

Little Nettie was among them, and when she saw the patch on Longtree's shoulder, she nearly had a heart attack. "Oh, no—not another one!" she screamed, turning and running out of the room.

Longtree was scared shitless. "I didn't do anything!" he said. "I'll leave right now if you want me to!"

Julie sat next to him. "That's all right, soldier. Don't worry about it."

A whore named LouAnn sat down on the other side of him. "Calm down," she cooed. "Everything's gonna be A-okay."

"What the hell's the matter with her?" Longtree asked.

"Well," said Julie, "that little girl's had a bad night."

"What happened?"

"Well, it seems that a couple of men from your division came in here and started some trouble. The first one tried to drag her out of here and then killed one of our bouncers with a knife, and then the second one threatened her with a bayonet."

"Golly," said Longtree, "that sounds awful."

"Yeah, the poor kid's really shaken up." Julie narrowed her eyes and looked him up and down. "You're not going to go crazy up here, are you?"

"Hell no," Longtree said. "Not me. Live and let live, that's what I always say. I'd go a mile out of my way to avoid trouble. In fact, if you're a little scared about me, I'll leave right now."

Julie leaned over and slipped her fingers between the buttons of his shirt, massaging his chest. "You wouldn't happen to have a knife on you by any chance?" she asked, gazing into his eyes for the lie.

"No, ma'am. You can search me if you want. What the hell would I be carrying a knife for? The only thing I brought up here with me is my dick."

She winked. "You wanna go to bed?"

"Yes, ma'am."

"My name's Julie."

"Yes, ma'am."

"What's your name?"

"Just call me Longtree."

"You're an Indian, ain't you?"

"Yes, ma'am, but I'm not one of them wild Indians. I'm a real calm Indian. I don't want no trouble."

"That's good," she said, "because I don't want any trouble either." She stood up and held out her hand. "Let's go."

"Yes, ma'am."

Longtree held her hand and she led him out of the room. In the corridor they walked hand in hand toward her workshop. Longtree didn't think she was the prettiest whore, but he was spooked by the situation and wanted to get alone with a woman—any woman—before any problems developed.

"Nervous?" she asked.

"No, ma'am."

"Yes you are. I can feel you shaking."

Longtree didn't know what to say, because he *was* shaking a little. But it wasn't fear. He hadn't been laid for a long time and couldn't wait to get started. She came to her room and opened the door, and he followed her inside.

"Well," she said with a smile, "what do you want?"

"I just wanna get laid, that's all."

"Five dollars for a straight lay, seven-fifty for a half-and-half, and ten for a full blowjob."

Longtree reached into his pocket and peeled five one-dollar bills off his roll. "I just want a straight lay," he said. "I don't go in for that funny stuff."

She laughed as she accepted the money. "Anything you say, soldier. I'll be right back. You can take your clothes off."

"Yes, ma'am."

She walked out the door and Longtree sat down on the chair, relieved that everything was going so well. He unlaced his shoes, took them off, and peeled away his khaki socks. Standing, he unknotted his necktie, unbuttoned his shirt, and took it off, revealing his bronzed body, covered with scars. The ugliest scar was on his back, where he'd been shot in the fight for the Gifu Line on Guadalcanal.

Julie returned to the room, took off her white cocktail dress, and walked toward the sink. She was dumpy and flabby, and her tits sagged badly, but she was a woman and that was good enough for Longtree.

"C'mere and let me look at your cock," she said.

"Yes, ma'am."

"You don't have any funny diseases, do you?"

"Oh, no, ma'am."

"You sure?"

"Yes, ma'am."

She got down on her knees and examined his cock, squeezing it to see if anything came out, twisting it around so she could look at its underside.

"You look fine," she said.

She filled up the sink with warm water, and Longtree recalled what the whores had said about the two soldiers from the Eighty-first Division who'd made trouble in the whorehouse earlier that night. As far as Longtree knew, he, Butsko, Bannon and Frankie LaBarbara were the only soldiers from the Eighty-first Division in Honolulu, because the Eighty-first was stationed on Guadalcanal and furloughs were hard to get. He and the others got theirs only as a reward for the reconnaissance job they'd done on the Jap-held island of New Georgia. Of course, a few other soldiers from the Eighty-first might have earned furloughs, too, but he couldn't help wondering if Butsko, Bannon, or Frankie La Barbara could have got into the trouble. They were all wild guys, and Longtree knew they were capable of anything.

"Say, there," Longtree said as Julie washed his cock, "did you happen to see those two guys who made the trouble here tonight?"

"I sure did."

"Do you know their names by any chance?"

"Why—you think you might know them?"

"I might."

She stopped washing his cock and froze, stiff as a board. "If they were your friends, are you going to go crazy?"

"I told you I'm not that kind of Indian."

"Are you sure?"

"Sure I'm sure. What do I have to do to prove it?"

She wagged her finger at him. "You'd better not start any shit."

"Don't worry about it."

"Well," she said, pulling his cock out of the water and patting it with a towel, "we don't know the second one's name, but the first one, the one who killed one of our bouncers, was named Bannon."

Longtree nearly collapsed onto the floor. His jaw fell open and he staggered to the bed, sitting down heavily, his back slumped, completely devastated. "Oh, shit," he said. "I knew it. I just knew it."

"He was a friend of yours!"

"Yes, ma'am. He was my squad leader."

She looked at him fearfully. "Are you all right."

He nodded. She could see that he was very unhappy. He didn't look like the kind of man who would go berserk. It was as if he'd just found out that a close relative had died. He looked up at her with melancholy eyes.

"You say he killed somebody?"

"I'm afraid so." She sat down next to him on the bed and put her arm around his shoulder to comfort him.

"How'd it happen?"

She explained how Bannon wanted to take Nettie out of the whorehouse, and about the subsequent bloody fight.

"Oh, no," Longtree said, shaking his head slowly from side to side. "This can't be."

"I'm afraid it really happened," Julie said.

"Where is he now?"

"The main Honolulu jail."

"What was the other one's name?"

"We didn't get his name," Julie said, "but he was an Italian-looking guy, an inch or two shorter than you. A real fast-talker."

Longtree closed his eyes and groaned, because that was a perfect description of Frankie La Barbara.

"And he had a big roll of money with him—claimed he won it all in a poker game."

Now Longtree knew it was Frankie for sure. "What'd he do?"

"Well, he didn't kill anybody or anything like that. He just put a bayonet against Nettie's throat and scared the shit out of her."

"Thank God he didn't do anything," Longtree said. His hard-on had gone limp and he didn't feel like screwing anymore. "I need a cigarette."

"Have one of mine."

They took cigarettes from her pack and he lit them with his Zippo. "You're not gonna believe this," he said, "but they're both good men. I don't know what happened. Maybe both of them were in combat too long. They've been through a lot." He puffed the cigarette. "Listen, I'd better get going. Maybe I can get Bannon out of jail."

93

"Not at this time of night you won't." Julie grabbed his dick and squeezed gently. "You won't be able to see him in the morning, so why don't you relax?"

"I can't relax. My squad leader is in the hoosegow."

"You can't relax?"

She held her cigarette high in the air and bent over, placing Longtree's flaccid cock in her mouth. Longtree felt his spine unravel suddenly, and the room spun around. He tried to think of Bannon and Frankie La Barbara, but somehow he couldn't. Julie was moaning softly, licking and slurping, and he was getting hard again. He lay back on the bed and stared at the ceiling as her head bobbed up and down.

"I thought you said you didn't like fancy stuff," she said, although her mouth was full.

Longtree sighed and closed his eyes. After all those lonely months on Guadalcanal he was finally getting some sex. He'd worry about Bannon tomorrow; now he had to take care of himself.

"Don't stop," Longtree whispered, wiggling his hips. "Just keep on going."

EIGHT . . .

It was morning on Guadalcanal, and Colonel Stockton walked across the clearing to his headquarters building. The sun was low on the horizon, and the troops in Headquarters Company were doing their calisthenic drill on the other side of the clearing. A pfc. walked toward him and threw a salute, and Colonel Stockton saluted back as he climbed the stairs to his headquarters, a small one-story wooden structure not far from Henderson Field. He pushed open the door and entered the orderly room, where Sergeant Major Ramsay sat behind his desk. Sergeant Major Ramsay looked up at Colonel Stockton over his reading glasses; he didn't look happy.

"We've got a problem, sir," he said.

"What is it?" Colonel Stockton asked, taking off his green fatigue hat with the silver eagle pinned on front.

Sergeant Major Ramsay stood and handed Colonel Stockton a document. It was a teletype message from the Provost Marshal of Schofield Barracks in Hawaii, advising Colonel Stockton that Butsko and Bannon were in the Honolulu jail pending trial.

Colonel Stockton turned pale. "Good grief!"

"They haven't even been gone twenty-four hours," Sergeant

Major Ramsay said, shaking his head sadly.

Colonel Stockton sat on the chair beside Sergeant Major Ramsay's desk and read the message again. Bannon was charged with manslaughter, and Butsko with aggravated assault. An officer from the judge advocate general's corps at Schofield Barracks would represent them. Colonel Stockton would be kept apprised of the proceedings.

Colonel Stockton sighed. "I was afraid something like this would happen. That goddamned recon platoon of mine just can't stay out of trouble."

"They're sure a tough bunch, sir."

"Bunch of damned hotheads—that's what they are." Colonel Stockton was getting angry, because this was one more thing to worry about, and he had enough to worry about as it was. Also, when a soldier killed a civilian, it was bad publicity for the Army and a reflection on the soldier's commmanding officer. It was unfair, but that's the way it worked. Colonel Stockton didn't need this now that he was up for his star.

Colonel Stockton stood and straightened his back, walking toward his office. "If any new information comes in on this, let me know."

"Yes, sir."

Colonel Stockton entered his office, hung up his hat on the peg, and sat behind his desk. He took a pipe off his rack, filled it with Briggs smoking mixture, tamped it down, and lit it, filling the air around him with clouds of blue smoke.

He couldn't stop thinking of Butsko and Bannon. He knew that both of them were outstanding front-line soldiers, but the same qualities that made them outstanding soldiers—aggressiveness and unwillingness to back down from tough challenges—were the same qualities that had landed them in jail. They were fighting son of bitches no matter where they were. Colonel Stockton knew them well enough to suspect that they hadn't started the trouble. Somebody else must have started it, and they had finished it in their usual bloody fashion.

He wondered about the two other men, Frankie La Barbara and Sam Longtree, who also were in Honolulu. *I hope they stay the hell out of trouble,* Colonel Stockton thought. *All I need is for them to wind up in jail too.* He scowled and drummed his fingers on his desk. *I probably should go to Honolulu myself to see what I can do. After all, I can't let those damned civilians railroad one of my men into the electric chair.*

Bannon lay on a slab of wood in the basement of the Honolulu jail. He was alone in a tiny cell furnished only with a wooden cot and a commode that stank to high heaven. A corridor passed by the bars in front of his cell, and the bare light bulbs in the corridor had been on all night. There were no windows anywhere, no ventilation, and the basement was warm and smelly from the odor of men's bodies and stinky commodes. Guards passed by occasionally, looking into the cells. Men coughed, farted, and swore all around the cellblock. Bannon couldn't see into any other cells, but he'd heard them filling up all through the night.

He lay on his back with his head on his hands and was completely disgusted with himself. He knew that he never should have made a scene in that whorehouse the night before, but it was too late now. He never should have insisted that the whore leave with him, but he'd been drunk and obsessed with the thought of saving her.

What's the matter with me? he thought. *Am I crazy?* He was actually worried that he didn't have all his marbles, because only a lunatic would do what he had done. The girl was a whore and he wanted to marry her. Now that he was sober and penned up like an animal, he realized how idiotic he'd been, especially when the bouncers arrived. He just should have walked the hell out of there.

But there was something about the whore that had touched his soul. She'd seemed so sweet and angelic. How could he not want to save her? How could any man walk away from such a tragic person? A man had to stand for something in his life. A man couldn't look the other way when he was in the presence of someone needy.

He laughed sardonically. *Am I just bullshitting myself?* he thought. Every whore in the Curtis Hotel was needy, but he didn't feel compelled to save any of them. Why did he want to save Nettie? Was it because she was prettier than the others, and a great fuck? Was he being a good guy, as he liked to think, or had he just been horny and selfish?

Bannon sat up and buried his face in his hands. It was all

97

so confusing, and he was getting a headache. But in one area there was no confusion: He was charged with manslaughter and would probably do a long stretch in prison. He had disgraced his name and his family. When Sergeant Butsko and the others found out about it, they'd really think he was an asshole. *How different my life would be if I hadn't gone to that whorehouse, or if I had screwed some other whore, or if I'd never tried to take Nettie out of there. If only I could go back and do it all over again.*

"All right—everybody out!" shouted a voice in another part of the cellblock.

"Exercise hour!" said another voice.

Doors clanged open and men grumbled and moved out. The guards kept hollering and finally they came into the corridor where Bannon was. One of them opened his door and he stepped out into the corridor, taking a look at his jailbird companions for the first time; they were a bunch of drunken old bums. He saw a couple of military uniforms in the dim light, but it never occurred to him that somebody he knew was in the Honolulu jail.

Bannon stumbled with the rest of them through the corridors toward an open door that led to the exercise yard. He stepped outside and the bright sun almost blinded him. The night before, when they booked him, they took away his Zippo lighter but let him keep his cigarettes. If he wanted a light, he'd have to ask for one, so he took a cigarette out of his pack, put it in his mouth, and walked toward one of the guards.

"Gimme a light," Bannon said.

The guard took out his lighter and flicked it. Bannon puffed his cigarette to life and filled his lungs with the smoke. It made him a little dizzy, and his heart beat faster, but it was just what he needed. As he was walking away he felt a hand on his shoulder.

He turned around and found himself looking at the bruised face of Sergeant Butsko! Bannon blinked, because he thought he might be hallucinating. Butsko had an expression of astonishment on his face.

"What the hell are *you* doing here!" Butsko demanded.

Bannon shook his head and groaned. "I'm in big trouble, Sarge. I killed a guy last night."

Butsko looked at Bannon as if Bannon had horns growing out of his forehead. "You *killed* a guy?"

"Yup."

"Jesus," Butsko said, "I wouldn't be surprised if Frankie La Barbara was in here for killing a guy, but not you. What happened?"

"The guy pulled a knife on me, and I just happened to be carrying a knife of my own."

"Were there any witnesses?"

"Lots, but I think they were all friends of the guy I killed."

"You might be able to get off."

Bannon shrugged. "I don't know. Nothing like this ever happened to me before. What are you in for?"

Butsko scowled. "I got into a brawl with a bunch of guys."

"Who started it."

"I think they did, and they think I did."

"Any witnesses?"

"A shitload, but everybody was drunk and it was a big mess."

"Anybody got hurt bad?"

Butsko nodded grimly. "I think so."

"Shit," Bannon said.

Butsko wheezed. "I know what you mean."

"What'll happen now?"

"I imagine we'll be arraigned pretty soon. The Army will furnish us a lawyer from the Advocate General's Corps, and he'll probably be a nitwit. All we can do is hope for the best. "Gimme one of your straights, will you, kid? I'm all out."

"Sure thing, Sarge."

Bannon took out his pack of cigarettes and held them up. Butsko took one and Bannon gave him a light from the end of his cigarette. Butsko puffed his cigarette and looked at Bannon as other prisoners shuffled around the compound or lay in the sun.

"Kid," Butsko said, "I'm afraid you're in a lot of trouble. I might wind up doing some time, but you might get a lot of time. You'd better get ready for the worst."

"I'm ready," Bannon said.

"In the long run you might be better off than the rest of us, because we'll probably wind up dead on some fucked-up island,

99

whereas you'll just be doing time someplace."

"I don't know," Bannon told him. "I think I'd rather be dead than do a lot of time."

Butsko shrugged. "Well, it depends on the lawyer the Army gives us. If he's good, we'll be okay, and if he's a bum, it won't go easy for us. All we can do is take it like it comes."

"I did what I thought I had to do at the time," Bannon said. "I'm a grown man. I'll take whatever medicine they give me."

Butsko looked at Bannon for a few moments, then smiled and slapped him on the shoulder. "You're okay, Bannon," he said. "No matter what happens, they'll never break you."

"Fucking A," Bannon said.

In another part of the jail, Frankie La Barbara and Dolly sat in a room lined with chairs, waiting to see Butsko. Other friends and relatives of prisoners also were in the room, waiting for their names to be called. In front of the room was a counter, behind which was an office area where people worked at desks. A uniformed man sat at the counter, reading the morning paper.

Frankie and Dolly were also reading the morning paper, and on the front page was the story about Bannon killing the bouncer in the whorehouse. The news photographer had taken a picture of Bannon when he'd been booked, and the story implied that Bannon had gone berserk in the whorehouse.

"This is bullshit," Frankie muttered. "Bannon's the sanest guy you ever wanna meet. The other guy must've egged him into it."

Dolly nodded as she read the newspaper story. The bruises on her face were covered with makeup and she was wearing her best clothes, plus too much jewelry and a perfume that was causing Frankie La Barbara to have occasional impure thoughts.

The man behind the counter called somebody's name, and a tearful old woman who was stooped over shuffled to the counter. The man opened a door in the counter and the woman stepped into the office area. Two guards were there and took her off to the visiting room.

Frankie looked at his watch. They'd been there a half hour already. "I wonder how long this is going to take?" he asked.

"Usually a couple of hours," Dolly said.

At that moment Longtree walked into the waiting room,

taking off his hat and trying to appear harmless, looking around to figure the place out. He and Frankie spotted each other at the same moment, and he walked toward Frankie, who stood up.

"Well," said Frankie. "I guess you heard the bad news."

Longtree nodded. "Yeah, I went to the Curtis Hotel and found out that Bannon killed somebody."

"I guess you ain't heard about Butsko yet."

"What did he do?" Longtree asked.

"He *nearly* killed about a half-dozen guys."

Longtree groaned.

Frankie turned to Dolly. "Let me introduce you to Mrs. Butsko."

"Mrs. Butsko?" Longtree asked.

"That's me," said Dolly.

Longtree smiled nervously. "I'm Pfc. Longtree."

Frankie pointed his thumb at Longtree. "He's the point man in the platoon."

"Hello," said Dolly, with a friendly smile.

Longtree shuffled his feet and bowed awkwardly. "Hello, ma'am."

An Army officer entered the waiting room, carrying an old leather briefcase. He had a pudgy face, eyeglasses as thick as the bottoms of Coke bottles, and thin, wiry hair. He walked up to the counter and said to the man in the uniform: "Hello, there. I'm the attorney of record for two soldiers incarcerated here, and I'd like to see them."

"Your name?" asked the clerk.

"Captain George Ginsberg."

"Your clients?"

"Sergeant John Butsko and Corporal Charles Bannon, US Army."

"Have a seat, Captain."

Ginsberg looked at his watch. "I don't have much time."

"There are two people ahead of you, but as the attorney of record you'll go first. I'll call you as soon as your prisoners are in the visiting room."

"Can I see them both at the same time?"

"Yes, sir."

Ginsberg turned to walk away and found himself looking

at Frankie La Barbara, who was examining him sharply.

"Hi, there," Frankie said. "You're gonna defend Butsko and Bannon?"

"Who're you?"

"I'm a friend of theirs and they're both innocent. They both did what they did in self-defense."

"Oh, yeah?" asked Ginsberg. "Do you have witnesses?"

"One of them's sitting right over there."

Ginsberg looked in the direction Frankie indicated and saw Dolly looking up at him over the top of her newspaper. Longtree was seated next to her. Ginsberg had practiced criminal law in Los Angeles before being drafted into the Army, and had met a lot of strange people in the course of his career. Nothing fazed him anymore.

"Let's go talk to her," Ginsberg said.

Frankie led Ginsberg over and introduced him to Dolly and Longtree. Ginsberg sat down and Dolly gave him a quick synopsis of the battle that had taken place in her home the previous evening.

Ginsberg made notes on his yellow notepad. "Any other witnesses besides you who'll testify that it was self-defense?" he asked.

"Yes," she replied.

"Any who'll say it wasn't?"

"Maybe," she said.

"Somebody'll have to talk with those people," Ginsberg said.

"Longtree and I'll talk to them," Frankie said ominously.

"What's the story with this Bannon guy?" Ginsberg asked.

Frankie told him all the details that he'd found out, omitting the part about holding a knife to Nettie's throat.

"Do you think any of those people will testify that it was self-defense?" Ginsberg asked.

"I think we can work that out," Frankie replied.

NINE . . .

That afternoon Nettie left the whorehouse to buy some cosmetics at the local drugstore. She also had to mail some letters to the folks back in South Carolina, and thought she'd take in a movie. She didn't have to be back to work until eight o'clock that night.

Nettie had many friends at the whorehouse, but never hung out with anybody. She lived in her own repressed dreamworld and hoped to have enough money saved in another two years to open a beauty parlor in Greensboro.

It was another sunny pleasant afternoon, and all the businesses in the neighborhood were open, taking servicemen's money. Men whistled at her but she just kept walking, because she was accustomed to attention from horny guys.

She became aware that somebody was walking beside her and turned to look. It was a woman, very busty, whose cosmetics unsuccessfully covered a black eye and other facial bruises.

"Can I have a word with you?" Dolly asked.

Nettie became frightened, because she tended to be paranoid, particularly after the events of the night before. "About what?" Nettie asked, acting tough, as she always did when she was scared.

"Listen," Dolly said, "there's a young soldier who's going to spend the rest of his life in jail unless you help him."

Nettie's hair nearly stood on end, because she knew what young soldier Dolly was referring to. "Listen," Nettie said, walking faster, "I don't want any trouble."

Dolly kept up with her and spoke in her most soothing voice. "He's been on Guadalcanal for almost a year and he's seen a lot of war. That bouncer pulled a knife on him and he reacted the only way he knew how."

Nettie remembered the scars on Bannon's body. "I don't know what I could do. I'm scared of him. He's crazy."

"He's not crazy," Dolly said. "He's just a lonely kid and he fell in love with you. He was drunk and he thought he was helping you. Then the bouncers came and everything got out of control."

"I don't want to have anything to do with this," Nettie said, holding her head high and crossing the street.

Dolly stayed at her side. "You can't let them put him away just because he was lonely and fell in love with you."

"He wasn't in love with me. He just wanted some free sex."

"That's not so. His buddies say he's honest and straight as an arrow. He's just been at the front too long, that's all, fighting for you and me and everybody else who's taking it easy in a safe place. He's fighting for you, so why can't you do something for him?"

On the other side of the street, Nettie stopped suddenly and looked at Dolly. "What do you want me to do?"

"Let's have a drink and talk about it. I'm buying."

"I really shouldn't," Nettie said, her voice trailing away.

"There's a war on and we have to do our part for the boys in uniform. This is something you can do personally."

"What are you to Bannon?" Nettie asked.

"My husband is a soldier, too," Dolly said, "and Bannon saved his life on Guadalcanal."

Nettie took a deep breath and her eyes darted around nervously as she thought of what to do. She was scared of Bannon and anyone who might know him, but she believed he was a decent guy underneath his craziness. She didn't want him to go to jail for the rest of his life.

"Okay," she said with a sigh. "Let's talk about it."

Frankie La Barbara walked into Ward 23-B at the Pearl Harbor Naval Hospital, wearing the white uniform of a hospital orderly. He snapped the fingers of his right hand and chewed gum as he looked around at the rows of soldiers lying in bed, their legs or arms suspended by traction, their heads bandaged, knocked out on drugs or just staring at the ceiling. Frankie realized that everybody in the ward was in pretty bad shape.

He bent down and looked at the names on the charts affixed to the beds. He was looking for Gunnery Sergeant Jack Crane, Dolly's former boyfriend, who was supposed to be in that ward, recuperating from injuries. Frankie wanted to have a little chat with him about his testimony in the trial to be held in two days.

Two nurses walked toward him, and he glanced up from the chart he was looking at to check them out. One was an adorable little blonde and the other a nice chubby brunette with big bouncy boobs. Frankie was tempted to make a pass at them but decided he'd better not take the chance. He had to stay as inconspicuous as possible.

The nurses walked by him and he continued looking at charts. On the other side of the aisle an orderly was making up an empty bed and looking at him suspiciously. Frankie pretended to be on a mission of the utmost importance as he moved along, hunched over, reading charts. Finally his eyes fell on the sign that said: CRANE, Jack R. G/Sgt.

Frankie straightened up and looked at his man. Crane's entire head was bandaged, leaving little holes for his eyes, mouth, and nose. His arm was in a sling and he was motionless. Frankie glanced around. The other orderly was absorbed with his bed-making, not paying any attention to Frankie. At the other end of the ward a doctor and nurse were examining a patient.

Frankie bent over Crane and whispered: "Hey!"

Crane didn't stir. Frankie called out to him again; still, there was no response.

"What's the problem over there!" shouted the orderly on the other side of the ward.

Frankie looked up. The orderly was staring at him. Frankie

pointed his thumb to his chest. "Me?"

"Don't bother that man!" the orderly said. "He's under heavy medication."

"Oh." Frankie walked toward the orderly. "There's some friends of his outside who want to visit him, and I wanted to see if he was okay."

"That man's not allowed to see visitors. He's too sick. He can't even talk because his jaw is broken. He's in bad shape—didn't you see his chart?"

"Yeah, but I thought I'd ask anyway." Frankie started backing away, smiling in his most ingratiating way. "If he's in bad shape, I guess he can't be interviewed or anything like that, huh?"

"Of course he can't be interviewed." The orderly narrowed his eyes at Frankie. "I don't think I've ever see you around here before. What's your name?"

"Joe," said Frankie, turning to walk away.

"Joe what?"

"Joe Bachegalupe. See you around."

"Wait a minute!"

Frankie walked swiftly out of the ward and entered the corridor that led to the next ward. The corridor was filled with doctors, nurses, orderlies, and patients, and he blended in with the scene. Glancing back, he couldn't see the orderly coming after him. The orderly probably figured there was no point in getting involved in something that might mean more work. Servicemen don't like to look for more work.

Rolling his shoulders, Frankie made his way toward the hospital exit, glad that he didn't have to threaten Jack Crane, because it would have been difficult to do in the ward with that orderly around. But Jack Crane wasn't in any condition to give testimony, even if it was a deposition taken at his bedside. Jack Crane would be out of the ballgame for a long time.

Frankie turned a corner and bumped into the cute blonde nurse he'd seen before.

"Hey," he said, taking a step backward, "how ya doing, sweetheart?"

She looked at him and he saw her eyes light up. Some women were attracted to him on first sight and some weren't, but this one evidently was.

"I'm not your sweetheart," she said gruffly, trying to walk around him.

He got in front of her, because he could perceive that she was acting. "I know you're not my sweetheart," he said, "but I sure wish you were. What time you go off duty?"

"None of your business. Get out of my way, please, or I'll call for the guards."

Frankie moved to the side, did an about-face, and walked beside her. "Please," he said, "don't do this to me. I think you're terrific. Let's have a drink together when you get off duty."

"I don't go out with sailors," she said, holding her nose high in the air.

"I ain't a sailor."

She glanced at him. "No? Then what are you?"

"I'm your slave, baby. Why don't you meet me when you go off duty and I'll do anything you say. I've got five hundred dollars in my pocket and we can really paint the town."

She stopped and looked up at him with her beautiful baby-blue eyes. "Where'd you get five hundred dollars?" she asked with a smile.

"I won it in a card game."

"I don't believe you."

"I'll show it to you."

Frankie looked around and saw a door that led to a flight of stairs. He motioned with his head and walked toward it, and the blonde nurse followed him. He opened the door and she proceeded to the landing, turning around and looking back at him.

He let the door close and took his roll out of his pocket. He unfolded it and flipped through the bills so she could see the tens and twenties. "Wanna hold it?" he asked.

"I've always had a weakness for Italian guys with black wavy hair," she replied.

"What time you go off duty?"

"Six o'clock."

"I'll meet you at the main gate."

"Okay." She turned to walk away, then stopped and looked at him again. "What's your name?"

"Frankie. Who're you?"

"Janie."

"See you later, Janie."

"Okay, Frankie."

Marie left first, and Frankie waited a few moments before he entered the corridor. He turned toward the exit and walked along swiftly, whistling a tune. *Funny how it works,* he thought. *Some of them won't talk to you even if you stand on your head, and others practically fall into your lap.* And the best part of it is that you didn't have to worry about getting the clap or the syph, because she was a nurse and nurses were clean.

In another part of the hospital Longtree was strolling through Ward 12-D, looking at the charts at the ends of the beds. Like Frankie La Barbara, he was dressed in a stolen orderly's uniform and trying to be inconspicuous. Doctors and nurses passed by, and on the other side of the ward an orderly was giving a shot to a patient.

The men in this ward weren't hurt so badly, and they were playing cards or checkers, reading magazines, and shooting the shit with each other. They didn't pay any attention to Longtree, and finally he came to an empty bunk whose chart was headed by the name: CHERNOV, Robert K. Sgt.

"Where's Sergeant Chernov?" Longtree asked.

"In the solarium," replied the man in the next bed.

"Thanks."

Longtree straightened up and walked to the ward solarium, at the end of the building. He left the ward, passed through a corridor lined with doors, and saw doctors and nurses in some of the rooms, examining patients. Some of the doors were closed; one of them led to the shithouse. He walked by the nurses' station and saw the light at the end of the corridor, where the solarium was. Quickening his pace, glancing around to make sure no one was looking at him too intently, he walked into the solarium and saw a group of men in a corner, listening to a radio; a few groups of card players; some chess and checkers players; and men reading magazines. The solarium had open windows on three sides, making everything bright and airy.

"Sergeant Chernov in here?" Longtree asked.

A man with a bandaged eye and hand turned around. "Yo!" he said.

"I've got to give you a test, Sergeant. Would you come with me, please?"

Sergeant Chernov stood and limped toward Longtree. "What kind of test?"

"Blood test."

"I already had a blood test today."

"You're gonna get another one."

"I'm startin' to feel like a goddamn pin cushion."

Longtree led the way down the corridor as Sergeant Chernov limped to stay up with him, wheezing and coughing, because Butsko had landed a haymaker on his throat during the big brawl. Longtree looked from side to side, trying to find someplace quiet. He saw an empty room with a scale and an examining table. "In here," he said.

Sergeant Chernov scuffled into the room behind him, and Longtree closed the door, latching it. Then he turned around and looked at Sergeant Chernov hobbling to the examining table.

"Where do you want it?" Sergeant Chernov asked. "Out of my arm or out of my ass?"

"Out of your guts," Longtree said in a deadly voice.

Sergeant Chernov blinked and turned around like an old man, although he was only twenty-nine. His eyes widened at the pearl handled jackknife in Longtree's hand, and all his wounds suddenly throbbed with pain.

"What's going on?" he asked through a constricted throat.

"Butsko's a friend of mine," Longtree told him, "and he's got a lot of other friends who'll do anything for him, and I mean anything. When you testify you'd better say that Sergeant Crane started the fight, not Butsko. Or else. Understand?"

Sergeant Chernov looked at the knife. "Sergeant Crane's got a lot of friends too."

"Fuck him and fuck his friends," Longtree said. "You're going to die if you don't do as I say, and don't forget, we know where to find you, but you don't know where to find us. Got it?"

Sergeant Chernov thought for a few moments. If this Indian could get to him in the hospital, so could somebody else. And besides, Sergeant Crane *had* thrown the first punch.

"I got it," he said.

"Good," Longtree replied, backing toward the door. "I'll see you around."

"I hope not," Chernov told him.

"You know what you gotta do," Longtree said, opening the door.

Longtree slipped into the corridor and walked away swiftly, threading his way through nurses and orderlies, passing a man in a wheelchair with a bottle of yellow liquid hanging above his head.

It was three o'clock in the afternoon in the Curtis Hotel, and the madam, Vivian Brill, sat in her office, going over the books. She sipped a glass of wine and wore her eyeglasses low on her nose as she read the column of numbers and saw all the money the whorehouse was making. Even on such a slow week, business was still good, and at the end of the month it would almost be like having a license to print money. She examined the totals to see which girls were making the most money, and as usual Trixie, Nettie, and a girl named Flo were at the top of the list.

There was a knock on the door.

"Who is it?" Mrs. Brill asked.

"Nettie."

"Come in, dear."

Vivian scratched her head as the door opened and Nettie entered, followed by another woman. Vivian had noticed lately that often she'd think things and then they'd happen. Just now she'd been thinking about Nettie and sudenly there she was. *Maybe I'm getting to be psychic,* Vivian thought. She looked at Dolly and figured she was a whore. *I got the picture,* Vivian thought. *This babe is a friend of Nettie's and Nettie wants me to give her a job.*

"Have a seat," Vivian said, "What can I do for you?"

Nettie smiled, and Vivian couldn't help noticing how innocent she looked. "This is Dolly Butsko," Nettie said. "Dolly, this is Vivian Brill."

"Hello," said Vivian.

"Hi," replied Dolly.

"Well," Vivian said again, "what can I do for you?"

"It's about that Army corporal and Carl," Nettie said. Carl was the bouncer who'd gotten killed.

"What about them?" Vivian asked.

"I'm gonna testify that the corporal pulled his knife in self-defense," Nettie said, "'cause that's the way it happened, and I think all the other people here, including you, should do the same."

Vivian creased her brow. "What the hell are you talking about! We can't let soldiers walk in here and kill people!"

"But Carl pulled a knife first."

Vivian shook her head. "If that crazy son of a bitch soldier gets away with this, every other soldier in the Army will think he can come up here and pull a knife! We can't have that!"

"I don't care," Nettie said. "I'm gonna testify the truth."

"You'd better not," Vivian said.

"I told you what I'm gonna do, Mrs. Brill. You can fire me if you wanna, but that's what I'm gonna do."

Vivian pointed at Nettie. "You've got a lot of nerve, young lady! This whole damn thing wouldn't have happened if it weren't for you!"

Nettie pinched her lips together like a little girl being scolded. Dolly looked at Nettie and tried to figure her out, because she was like an eight-year-old girl and a grown woman rolled into one.

"I don't care what you say, Mrs. Brill," Nettie said. "I told you what I'm gonna do and I'll do it."

Vivian Brill reached for her pack of cigarettes and lit them up, her hands trembling. On one hand she wanted to fire Nettie, but on the other, Nettie was one of her best workers. No servicemen ever complained about Nettie, and this was the first trouble Nettie had ever had in the year since she'd been at the Curtis Hotel. Then Vivian became aware of Dolly, sitting back on the sofa as if she owned the joint. Had Dolly put a bug in Nettie's mind about this?

Vivian looked at Dolly. "What's all this to you?"

Dolly looked Vivian in the eye. "That soldier who you call a crazy son of a bitch saved my husband's life on Guadalcanal—that's what it's to me." Dolly sat straighter. "And let me tell you something: You wouldn't be sitting where you are right now if it weren't for men like my husband and soldiers like the one you call a crazy son of a bitch. Those soldiers are fighting for you and me and all Americans, and although they might be just a bunch of johns to you, they're American fighting men to me." Dolly's voice became stronger as her anger boiled more furious. "That bouncer of yours wasn't a soldier. He was just a dirty little back-stabber, but that young corporal had spent nearly a year on Guadalcanal, and he wasn't about to back down before some dirty little back-stabber. I don't care whether a woman is a whore or a madam or whatever she does—all of us should stand behind our men in uniform, especially people like you who earn your living off them."

Vivian Brill was a tough old broad herself, and nobody intimidated her. "No soldier's gonna come into my place and make trouble, and I don't give a shit where he's been or what he's done."

"But Mrs. Brill," Nettie said, "Carl pulled a knife first."

"And don't forget," Dolly added, "that Bannon is a combat soldier, and when he sees a knife he just goes into action. That's what his training is for. He don't know any different."

Vivian Brill scowled. "I've got to keep some standards here, otherwise servicemen will rip the place up."

Dolly leaned forward. "Let me tell you something, sweetheart. Bannon is a very popular man, and so is my husband. If you testify against Bannon, you're gonna have about a hundred soldiers from their outfit running through here one of these nights, and when they're finished there ain't gonna be anything left, and you might not even be left either."

Vivian thought of soldiers tearing the Curtis Hotel to shreds, and a shiver passed through her, but still she wouldn't give in. "I'll just call the MPs and have 'em all put away."

"Oh, yeah?" Dolly asked. "And how many servicemen do you think'll come up here after you do that? These guys are like brothers to each other when the chips are down, and they're not going to patronize a place that throws their buddies in jail and testifies against them in court, telling lies and stuff. This joint'll become a haunted house before you know it, 'but'— and now Dolly smiled—"if you tell the truth and testify that your bouncer pulled the knife first on Bannon, which is the way it happened, all the servicemen on Hawaii will find out about it within twenty-four hours, because news like that moves fast, and they'll think you're on their side and that the Curtis Hotel backs them up when they need to be backed up, and I wouldn't be surprised if you get more business than ever up here."

112

"Hmmm," said Vivian Brill. She looked down at her ledgers and saw all the money she was making. It would be a shame to place the business in jeopardy just because of a bouncer who had pulled a knife on a soldier. And if business improved, it would be wonderful. She puffed her cigarette and realized that the other things Dolly said were true too. American soldiers were fighting a war and they deserved a break every now and then. "Okay," she said, "I'll do it. I just don't want that Bannon, or anybody who knows him, in this establishment ever again. Is it a deal?"

"It's a deal," Dolly said.

Nettie jumped up, wrapped her arms around Vivian Brill's wrinkled throat, and kissed the thick layer of makeup on her cheek. "Oh, thank you so much, Mrs. Brill!" she said.

Vivian Brill was touched by the sudden show of emotion and was flustered. She pushed Nettie away and frowned. "You'd better go to your room and get ready for work."

"Yes, Mrs. Brill."

Nettie turned and ran out of the office, and Dolly arose from the sofa.

"Thanks a lot," Dolly said. "You won't regret it."

"I hope not," Vivian Brill said gruffly.

Dolly walked out of the office, and Vivian looked down at her ledgers but couldn't see the numbers because her eyes were misty. She remembered when she was young and had loved a man so much she would have done anything for him. He'd been killed in the First World War, and she'd gotten hard after that, but it was nice to see that other women could still care that way about men. Somebody had to, she supposed.

She wiped her eyes and the numbers came into focus. It sure wasn't easy to run a whorehouse. Crazy things happened all the time. But it was worth it, and Vivian Brill never let her emotions overrule her sound business sense.

Soldiers came and soldiers went, but the Curtis Hotel would remain forever if she had anything to say about it.

General Douglas MacArthur sat in his office on the eighth floor of the AMP Building in Brisbane, Australia. He was smoking a corncob pipe, and his battered old war-dog hat hung on a peg behind him. On the desk were the plans for Operation CARTWHEEL, comprising a systematic series of amphibious attacks throughout the Solomon Islands and New Guinea, culminating with an assault on the Japanese stronghold of Rabaul, on New Britain Island.

It was a massive operation, extremely complex because it required the coordination of huge numbers of troops, both Army and Marine, plus their air support, sea transport and seaborne artillery support. There were problems of command, because Admiral Nimitz would direct half of the operation and MacArthur would direct the rest. The logistical requirements were almost beyond comprehension.

General MacArthur looked at the maps and plans, his keen mind filing away facts and important information. His memory was legendary; he could read pages of information once and then recite them word for word, never making an error. His square jaw moved from side to side as he chewed the stem of his pipe and meditated on the coming battle.

He knew that when all was said and done, the Army and Marine infantry would have to do the dirty work. They'd have to take ground, hold it, and take more ground. Everything would depend on the individual foot soldier, and the outcome of Operation CARTWHEEL would depend on those faceless ordinary men, most of whom had been civilians when the Japs bombed Pearl Harbor.

General MacArthur knew that the fighting was going to be tough in the jungles of the Solomon Islands, and that the Japanese infantry soldiers were an elite, like the German infantry, whereas American infantrymen tended to be the dregs of the draftees after the Air Corps and Navy skimmed off the best for their technological specialities.

But General MacArthur knew that the American soldier was a fighting soldier when he had to be. He griped and goldbricked and went AWOL whenever he could, but when the chips were down the American soldier fought like a son of a bitch. He remembered how they'd battled on Bataan, when they'd been outnumbered and outgunned by the Japanese and weakened by short rations.

General MacArthur gritted his teeth, because Bataan was a bitter memory to him. He had been defeated by the Japanese, and it rankled. He was a proud man, the son of a general who won the Congressional Medal of Honor in the Civil War, and he himself had been one of the most decorated American soldiers of the First World War. Yet, the Japs had kicked him out of the Philippines, and all he wanted to do was return, just as he said he would.

Often he recalled his last days on Corregidor, when he had radioed General Marshall in Washington and told him of his plan to break his American soldiers out of the Japanese ring of hell on Bataan. He'd feint toward his left flank with a powerful artillery barrage and then attack on the right with the remainder of his II Corps, taking the enemy's Subic Bay positions in reverse, then follow with an assault by his I Corps. If successful, they'd capture enough supplies to carry on the fight, and they could escape into the Zambales Mountains, where they could carry on guerrilla warfare indefinitely. But General Marshall had turned him down, and his brave army was captured. Twenty-five thousand of his men became casualities and it all could have been avoided if Washington had listened.

There was a knock on his door and he looked at his watch. It was 1000 hours; General Oglesby was right on time as usual. "Come in!"

The door opened and General Oglesby marched into the office, carrying his briefcase. He came to a halt in front of General MacArthur's desk and saluted smartly. General MacArthur returned the salute.

"Have a seat, General."

"Yes, sir."

General Oglesby sat down and opened his briefcase, taking out a sheaf of papers. General MacArthur pushed the Operation CARTWHEEL plans to the side and found the stack of personnel information on colonels in his command who were eligible for the two brigadier stars that he could award.

"Well," said General MacArthur, "I imagine you've had more time to go over the records of these officers than I. Do you have any recommendations?"

"They're all good men," General Oglesby replied, "and I'm sure every one of them deserves a star, but unfortunately they all can't get one. I'd say the men most qualified are Colonel William Stockton, who commands the Twenty-third Regiment on Guadalcanal, and Colonel Dale Herkimer, who's on General

Kruger's staff at Sixth Army. Stockton is a field commander and Herkimer is a staff man. I think they'll make two good, balanced choices."

"Herkimer is fine with me," General MacArthur said, "but I think Stockton needs a little more time in grade."

"But sir," said General Oglesby, "he's got more time in grade than Herkimer."

General MacArthur shook his head. "I'm afraid this isn't going to be Colonel Stockton's turn. Maybe next time, but not now."

"Would you tell me why you think that, sir?"

"Because he's too much of a hothead, and it shows in everything he does."

"A hothead, sir? But he's done a magnificent job on Guadalcanal. His regiment has won astounding victories, and they're always in the forefront of the fight. His casualties haven't been any higher than anyone else's, so what makes you think he's a hothead?"

General MacArthur smiled. "He's a friend of yours, isn't he?"

"Well, yes, we were classmates at West Point, but I also know Colonel Herkimer and several of the other officers on the list."

General MacArthur leaned back in his chair and hooked his thumbs in his belt. "I expect something special from my generals," he said. "I expect them to be outstanding in every way, because they're in the public eye more than other officers. To be blunt, I don't think Colonel Stockton has handled his personal life very well, and I don't think he handles his men very well. His wife has been such a scandal that even *I* know about her, and then a few days ago one of his men killed somebody in a house of ill repute in Honolulu, which was all over the papers, even here in Australia. It makes the Army look bad when something like that happens, and I always say that trouble begins at the top. A good, solid officer has good, solid men. If a man from the Twenty-third Regiment killed a man in a whorehouse in Honolulu, I say that Colonel Stockton is lacking in leadership. I may be wrong, but that's the way I feel. Perhaps if I had more stars to award, I'd give him one anyway, because I agree, he *has* done a fine job on Guadalcanal. But until then, I'd like to give this one to a good field commander whose personal life isn't a mess and whose men haven't killed anybody in any brothels. Who's next on your list?"

"Colonel Shanks, sir."

General MacArthur turned down the corners of his mouth. "Shanks is a good man. Give the star to Shanks."

"Yes, sir."

"And if Colonel Stockton does a good job in the future, and keeps his men out of trouble, and behaves himself, maybe he'll get the next star. You can tell him that if you want to, since he's a friend of yours."

"Yes, sir."

TEN . . .

"This court will come to order!" said the black-robed judge, pounding his gavel three times. "Bailiff, read the charges!"

The stout bailiff stood beside the judge's desk. "The people against Master Sergeant John Butsko, US Army, charged with aggravated assault."

"Proceed with the presentation of evidence!" declared the judge.

Captain Ginsberg shot to his feet and raised his hand. "May I approach the bench, Your Honor!"

The judge squinted at him through glasses that were even thicker than Captain Ginsberg's. "Who're you?"

"I am the attorney for the accused, Your Honor, and I have important information to relay to you immediately."

"But the trial hasn't even started yet!"

"It should not start, Your Honor, because the prosecution has no case!"

"That's not so, Your Honor!" shouted the prosecuting attorney, standing abruptly. He wore a dark blue suit and his name was Benjamin Goodall.

"Your Honor," Captain Ginsberg said, "may I *please* approach the bench?"

The judge groaned. "All right," he said, and then he pointed to the prosecuting attorney. "You'd better come up here too."

Both men strolled toward the bench while the judge looked down at them harshly. Back in the courtroom, behind the defendant's table, Butsko groaned, because he'd noticed that his defense attorney, Captain Ginsberg, wore argyle socks with his uniform.

Dolly was seated next to Butsko at the table. Behind them were Longtree and Frankie La Barbara, plus a gathering of Dolly's friends, who would be witnesses for the defense, and some curious onlookers who liked to attend trials.

On the bench the judge crossed his arms and leaned forward, glaring through his glasses at Captain Ginsberg. "Well?"

"Your Honor," said Captain Ginsberg, "I've got five witnesses here who'll testify that the defendant fought in self-defense after being attacked in his own home."

The judge widened his eyes. "His own home, you say?"

"Yes, Your Honor, his own home, after he had returned on furlough from Guadalcanal, where he had been in nearly continuous combat for a year and where he won the Silver Star for bravery in the face of the enemy. Your Honor, this man is one of the most distinguished soldiers in the US Army, he has an outstanding combat record, and he is one of the few survivors of the Bataan Death March. Surely you've heard of the Bataan Death March, Your Honor."

"Indeed I have," said the judge, looking at Butsko with new respect.

"Since he was attacked in his own home," Captain Ginsberg continued, "and I have witnesses to testify to that, and in view of his military record, I request herewith that all the charges against him be dropped."

The judge turned to the prosecuting attorney, Mr. Goodall. "What do you have to say about this?"

"Your Honor," Goodall said, "I don't think we should let sentiment or patriotism sway us from our duty here. The people will prove that the defendant has a brutal and vicious nature and that the violence in his home erupted over his wife, who is a lady of highly questionable character."

"I object!" Captain Ginsberg shouted. "Mrs. Butsko is not on trial here!"

"You can't object," the judge said dryly. "The trial hasn't even started yet."

"But Mrs. Butsko isn't on trial."

"Of course she's not on trial," the judge agreed.

"But," said the prosecutor, "her behavior is germane to the case."

The judge looked at the prosecutor with annoyance. "The defense alleges that you have no witnesses. Is that correct?"

"Two days ago I had witnesses, Your Honor, but since then they've all changed their stories. I have reason to believe that they've been intimidated."

Captain Ginsberg turned red with rage. "This is an outrage, Your Honor! The prosecution is making wild allegations with no basis in fact! If he has no witnesses, he should say so without making allegations."

A door opened at the rear of the courtroom, and everyone turned around at the sound. A tall, lean, silver-haired officer entered the courtroom, and Butsko's eyes nearly popped out when he saw that it was Colonel Stockton, attired in a tailored and starched tan Class A uniform, his insignia gleaming on his collar, his combat ribbons lined up over his left breast pocket, and above them all the Combat Infantryman's Badge.

The judge was impressed, as any aging, overweight, sedentary man would be by the sight of a man his own age who had such vigor and charisma. Colonel Stockton, holding his cunt cap in his hand, looked around and saw Butsko, who smiled weakly.

"May I help you, sir?" bellowed the judge.

"I have come here all the way from Guadalcanal," Colonel Stockton replied, "to testify on behalf of Master Sergeant Butsko, who is a member of my regiment."

"Please approach the bench, sir."

Ramrod-straight, Colonel Stockton marched to the bench and stood erectly, at ease and yet at attention, alert and indomitable, the very model of a modern colonel of infantry.

"What can you tell us about the defendant?" the judge asked.

"He's one of the finest soldiers in my command," Colonel Stockton replied, "and he's one of the heroes of the Guadalcanal campaign. He's in charge of my reconnaissance platoon, and there were many close battles that could have gone the other way were it not for the courage and leadership ability of Sergeant Butsko. It is difficult for me to believe that such a man could be guilty of the charges placed against him here today."

"Hmmm," said the judge. "I see."

Captain Ginsberg pointed his finger in the air. "Let me point out, Your Honor, that there are precedents in the law for my request that you dismiss this case." He went on to describe various cases that were thrown out of court due to the lack of witnesses for the prosecution, but the judge wasn't listening; he was looking at Colonel Stockton and wondering how a man could be strong and vigorous at his age, while he, the judge, was flabby, tired, and cranky all the time. Colonel Stockton's presence intimidated him, and it particularly galled the judge to see all the combat ribbons on Colonel Stockton's chest, when all the judge had done in his life was hang around courtrooms.

Finally the judge could stand it no more. He felt he couldn't stand up to Colonel Stockton, Captain Ginsberg, and Sergeant Butsko. He raised his gavel in the air, slamming it down and interrupting Captain Ginsberg's speech.

"Case dismissed due to insufficient evidence!" the judge declared. "This court is adjourned."

The judge arose, gathered his black robes around him, and strode out of the courtroom, wondering where he'd gone wrong in life and why he was a pompous old fool instead of a real man like Colonel Stockton.

Butsko stood and kissed Dolly. Frankie La Barbara and Longtree crowded around and slapped Butsko on the back. Colonel Stockton walked by and gave Butsko a look that wiped the smile off Butsko's face. Colonel Stockton didn't hesitate; he just kept walking toward the door of the courtroom, and Butsko realized that Colonel Stockton was angry at him.

Something told him he might have been better off going to jail for a few years, rather than return to Colonel Stockton's Infantry Regiment on Guadalcanal.

In the afternoon Bannon sat in his cell, waiting to be taken to the courtroom for his trial. Captain Ginsberg had just left, after giving him a pack of cigarettes and telling him that Butsko's case had been thrown out of court. Ginsberg also told

Bannon that his case would probably go to a full trial, because manslaughter was a capital offense.

In addition, Bannon found out for the first time that Colonel Stockton would testify on his behalf and, more incredibly, so would Nettie and the women from the Curtis Hotel! Bannon was still reeling from that news. He puffed his cigarette and gazed at the stone wall facing him, thinking about Nettie and how terrified she had been of him. Captain Ginsberg told him that Butsko's wife had convinced Nettie to testify, and Bannon wondered how Butsko's wife had done it.

After a while he heard footsteps in the corridor. Two guards appeared in front of his cell.

"Let's go, Bannon," one of them said. "Trial time."

Bannon stood up as they unlocked the cell. They swung open the barred door and Bannon stepped out, hoping he'd never have to sit in that smelly cell again. Captain Ginsberg told him that he had a good chance of winning the case.

The guards escorted him through the labyrinthine corridors of the jail and up the stairs to the courthouse, where they traversed more corridors, finally arriving at the door of the courtroom. Two other guards opened the doors and Bannon walked inside.

The judge wasn't there yet, but the jury was seated and so were the prosecutor and Captain Ginsberg. The courtroom was full, because the case had received a lot of publicity in the newspapers. Butsko, Dolly, Longtree, Frankie La Barbara, Janie the nurse, and the women from the whorehouse were seated behind the defense's table. Bannon walked by and saw Nettie looking at him, a frightened expression on her face. Bannon smiled thinly and proceed to the defense table, where he sat beside Captain Ginsberg.

"Don't worry," Captain Ginsberg told him. "You can beat this rap."

Bannon looked at the jury, and the ten men and two women looked back at him. They saw a clean-cut young man wearing his Combat Infantryman's Badge and a row of ribbons, including a Purple Heart, which Captain Ginsberg told him to wear. Captain Ginsberg's strategy was to appeal to the patriotic sentiments of the jury, using Butsko and Colonel Stockton as character witnesses who'd say what a great soldier and All-American hero Bannon was. Then the women from the whorehouse would testify that Bannon acted in self-defense.

The prosecuting attorney, who looked like an undertaker and dressed like one, took his position at his table, opening his briefcase and pulling out handfuls of documents. The bailiff told everybody to stand, and the judge entered the courtroom. He was an elderly man with a bald, freckled head and wire-rimmed eyeglasses. Captain Ginsberg maneuvered to get this particular judge, whose name was Collins, because his oldest son, an ensign in the Navy, had been killed during the Japanese bombing of Pearl Harbor.

The judge called the courtroom to order and the bailiff read the charges. The trial began and the prosecutor made his introductory statement, which described Bannon as a psychotic killer who had knifed an innocent bystander in cold blood. He admonished the jury not to be influenced by Bannon's combat record and told them to bear in mind that Bannon had killed a civilian in a particularly brutal and bloody way.

Then Captain Ginsberg made his introductory statement and tore the prosecutor's argument to shreds. He cited Bannon's brilliant combat record and stated that the fine, noble young soldier seated next to him had nearly been killed on his first furlough by a drunken madman with a criminal record, which indeed the bouncer did have, and that it would be a crime to send such a decent young man to jail for defending himself.

Upon the conclusion of his own introductory statement, the prosecutor presented his case, which consisted mainly of statements by policemen who'd arrived on the scene of the crime after it was committed, and by lab technicians who had described how the bouncer had died. The prosecutor ended his statement by pointing to Bannon and asking: "If this defendant wasn't guilty, why did he attempt to escape from the scene of the crime? If he acted in self-defense, what was he afraid of?" Turning to the jury, he declared dramatically: "He ran away because he knew he'd killed a man in cold blood, he knew he was guilty, he knew he might get the electric chair, and he knew that his only chance was to flee like the guilty murderer that he was!"

"Why, you son of a bitch!" Frankie said, jumping to his feet. "You fucking..."

"Siddown!" Butsko yelled.

Frankie's mouth became paralyzed by fear of Butsko, and

slowly he sank back down into his chair, to be comforted by Janie the nurse, who had the day off from the hospital and had come to attend the trial.

The judge looked at his watch; it was three o'clock in the afternoon. "We'll take a thirty-minute recess now," he said, "and then we'll proceed with the presentation by the defense." He pounded his gavel, arose, and walked toward a side door.

Bannon looked at the jury and wondered what they were thinking. He thought the prosecutor had made a very convincing case against him. If he were on the jury, he'd send himself to prison for life, except that he knew he wasn't guilty and that the bouncer had pulled the knife on him first.

Captain Ginsberg placed his hand on Bannon's shoulder. "Don't worry. Everything's going to be all right."

Meanwhile, behind him, Nettie was sidestepping toward the aisle. She knew he was going to turn around and try to talk with her, and she didn't know what to say to him. The possible confrontation terrified her, and all she could do was flee, which was the way she'd dealt with personal problems all her life.

Bannon stood up to go after her, but Butsko loomed in front of him, holding Dolly's hand.

"Don't worry about a thing, kid," Butsko said. "You got a good mouthpiece and he'll get you off." He turned to Dolly. "Meet my wife. Dolly, this is Corporal Bannon."

Dolly smiled, and Bannon thought she was a wild-looking old babe. So this was the famous Dolly, the bane of Butsko's existence.

"Hello," he said.

"Hiya," she replied.

"Thanks for all you've done to get these witnesses here."

"A friend of Johnny's is a friend of mine."

The trial resumed after the recess, and Captain Ginsberg presented his case. He called Colonel Stockton and Sergeant Butsko to the stand, and both spoke of Bannon's sterling character, his gallantry under fire, his devotion to duty, etcetera. Butsko even described in glorious detail how Bannon had saved his life on Guadalcanal.

The prosecutor cross-examined both of them, trying to open holes in their testimony, but he got nowhere.

Then Captain Ginsberg brought Nettie to the stand, and she described in a halting voice how the bouncer had pulled a knife on Bannon first. She left out the part about Bannon trying to drag her out of the whorehouse, but on cross-examination, the prosecutor tried to elicit that information. Nettie stood her ground and insisted that she didn't remember exactly what Bannon had said, but that she'd called the bouncer because Bannon had been a little drunk and rowdy.

The prosecutor kept probing but got nowhere. Then, exasperated, he asked Nettie about her life in the whorehouse, trying to imply that her testimony was worthless since she was nothing but a whore. Captain Ginsberg objected to his line of questioning, calling it character assassination, and his objection was sustained.

The other whores and their madam, Vivian Brill, were called to the stand, and all of them testified that the bouncer had pulled the knife first. The prosecutor was unable to shake their testimony under cross-examination.

Finally Bannon was called to the stand. He was ready, because Captain Ginsberg had prepared him well. In response to Captain Ginsberg's questions, Bannon explained that he'd been a ranch foreman in Texas before the war and had no criminal record. He said that he'd enlisted in the Army after Pearl Harbor and fought on Guadalcanal since the initial US Army landings in October. The prosecutor objected to the testimony, stating that there was no need to know Bannon's life history, but his objection was overruled because the judge thought it was so interesting.

Then Ginsberg questioned Bannon about the events that had taken place in the whorehouse, and Bannon said that he'd drunk too much and blacked out for a short period of time. The bouncers had tried to throw him out and he had resisted, and then one of them pulled a knife and he had to defend himself. After he'd killed the bouncer he ran away because he was drunk and confused.

The prosecutor cross-examined Bannon, trying to plant the idea in the jurors' minds that he was nothing more than a criminal in uniform who'd killed a man in rage and cold blood, but his voice suggested he didn't really believe it himself. America was at war and even the prosecutor was a patriot. He felt intimidated by Bannon, who was fighting the enemy on the battlefield instead of trying to put people in jail. Bannon fended off his questions and finally the prosecutor gave up and rested his case.

The judge gave his instructions to the jury, and they filed out of the room. They deliberated for an hour; then their foreman sent word to the judge that they had reached a verdict.

Everyone returned to the courtroom, and the judge pounded his gavel. "The court will come to order!" he said. Then he turned to the jury. "Have you reached a verdict?"

"We have, Your Honor," said the foreman. "We find the defendent *not guilty!*"

Frankie La Barbara shouted for joy and threw his cunt cap into the air. The judge pounded his gavel and declared that the trial was over. He walked out of the courtroom as soldiers and whores crowded around Bannon, shaking his hand, slapping his back, thanking Captain Ginsberg for doing such a good job.

Nettie tried to get away, but this time Frankie La Barbara was ready for her, and he grabbed her arm. "Where are you going, baby?"

"Home," she said, trying to break loose from his iron grip.

"Don't you think you ought to congratulate the corporal for beating the rap."

"He's got enough people congratulating him."

"The more the merrier."

Frankie pulled her toward Bannon, and at that moment Bannon was able to see her through all the bodies crowding around him. Nettie felt her insides quaking, but she gritted her teeth and tried to pull herself together as Bannon approached.

"I'm sorry about everything," she said, looking at his shirt because she couldn't bring herself to look at his face.

"That's okay," Bannon replied. "It was my fault, I guess. Thanks for coming here and testifying for me."

She looked up at him, and her eyes filled with tears. "It was the least I could do."

"Don't cry," he said. "Everything's gonna be okay."

"Well, it's all so sad," she replied, looking away again.

"No it's not."

"Don't be so nice to me. You should hate me for what I did."

"I don't hate you. I could never hate you."

"You just scared me, that's all, when you started talking about marriage and that stuff."

"I'll still do it if you want."

"Naw, that's okay."

"Maybe you should think about it."

"I don't deserve somebody like you."

"I don't think I deserve somebody like you."

They looked at each other and moved closer. Then Colonel Stockton's voice boomed out.

"All furloughs in the Twenty-third Infantry Regiment are revoked as of right now!" he said angrily, and everyone turned to face him. "I want you four men on the next plane to Guadalcanal *or else!* Sergeant Butsko, make sure my orders are carried out! Report to Sergeant Major Ramsay as soon as you get back!"

"Yes, sir!" said Butsko, who feared Colonel Stockton more than any civilian court of law.

Colonel Stockton turned and marched out of the courtroom, and Butsko knew that he was very mad. He knew there'd be hell to pay when all of them returned to Guadalcanal.

"All right, you heard him!" Butsko said to Bannon, Longtree, and Frankie. "You've got fifteen minutes to finish up your business, and then we're leaving for Hickam Field!"

Frankie La Barbara turned to Janie, the little blond nurse. "Well, kid, I guess this is it," he said. "I'll see you again someday, I hope."

"Will you write to me, Frankie?" she asked.

"Sure," he said. "You know I will."

But both of them knew very well that he wouldn't.

A few feet away Butsko looked down at Dolly as spectators filled out of the courtroom.

"I wish I could stay a while longer," Butsko said, "but the Army is the Army."

"I can drive you to Hickam Field."

"No, because I'll have to take the men with me, and they'll want to take their girls with them, and there won't be room."

"Sure there'll be room," Dolly said. "We'll make room."

"I don't know," Butsko said. "You never know what might happen."

"It could be worse if you go out to Hickam Field in a bus."

Butsko let that roll over his mind. The bus would be full of drunken servicemen, and anything could happen. "Okay," he said. "We'll do it." He turned to his men. "Change of plans! We're leaving for Hickam Field right now in my wife's vehicle! Let's go!"

"Can I come?" asked Janie.

"Sure."

Bannon looked at Nettie. "Why don't you come too?"

"I don't know," she said nervously. "I have to be at work."

"You can be late one day. C'mon."

She wrinkled her nose, because she was shy and didn't want to be in a car full of strangers who knew she was a whore.

"Please," Bannon said.

She imagined him in his combat uniform, lying in a foxhole, fighting Japs. Maybe he wouldn't be alive much longer. It was the least she could do for the war effort.

"All right," she said.

They all left the courthouse and piled into Dolly's 1933 Chervolet sedan. Butsko drove, Dolly sat beside him, and Longtree was on the right end of the front seat, the only one without a girl. In the backseat Bannon and Nettie, and Frankie and Janie, smooched all the way through the streets of Honolulu and over the highway until they came to Hickam Field. Butsko pulled into the parking area next to the main gate and cut the engine.

"All right, let's hit it," he said.

They all got out of the car.

"Make it short," Butsko said.

Longtree stood to the side and watched the others say goodbye. He felt sad, because he wasn't as lucky as Bannon or as forward as Frankie or married, like Butsko. But there had been a time on Guadalcanal when they'd captured a Japanese comfort girl, and he was the one who'd wound up in her arms at night while the others slept alone.

"Dolly," Butsko said, his big hands on her waist, "stay out of trouble, willya?"

"I'll try, Johnny. You stay out of trouble too."

"Fat chance of that," Butsko replied, thinking of the upcoming campaign on New Georgia.

"Well, keep your head down, anyway."

"And you keep your pants on."

She blushed. "Oh, Johnny, we never had a chance to be alone."

"I'll see you again sometime, and if I don't, well, that's the way it goes."

She wrapped her arms around him and held him close to her. "You'll be back, Johnny. I'm not worried about that. You're too mean to die."

Nearby, Frankie kissed the red berry lips of Janie the nurse, and she was crying. "I'm going to miss you, Frankie," she whispered, "and I know you'll forget me in five minutes, because I'm just another girl to you, and you'll never love anybody but yourself."

Frankie did a double-take, because he knew she was absolutely right. Maybe he would remember her after all. "Baby," he said, "all I know is that this time tomorrow I'll be back on Guadalcanal, and a week from now I might have Japs shooting at me, but I'll remember you and your sweet little ass, don't you worry about it."

"Why is it," she sighed, "that I'm attracted to men who are no good for me?"

"Whataya mean?" Frankie asked. "What makes you think I'm no good for you? What'd I ever do to you?"

"You made me love you," she said. "Now I'll be sick for a year."

"Naw," Frankie said, "in a few days you'll meet another nice guy like me and you'll forget all about me."

"I'll never forget you, Frankie."

"Bullshit."

On the other side of the car, Bannon gazed into Nettie's eyes.

"I wish I didn't have to leave so soon," he said.

"I wish you didn't either."

"Maybe if I stayed around, someday you'd be able to trust me."

"I trust you right now."

"Do you really?"

She nodded and didn't look away this time. "Yes."

"I wish you weren't going back to the whorehouse," he said.

"I'll get out as soon as I can and get a defense job, like you said. You were right and I know it now. Being a whore is no good."

"Jesus, I wish we could get married," Bannon said, pressing his cheek against hers.

"When you come back to Honolulu someday, I'll be waiting for you. Then we can get married if you still want to."

"Of course I'll want to."

"Time makes people change their minds."

"I'm not changing my mind," Bannon said. "How'll I be able to find you?"

"Give me your address. I'll write to you."

Bannon took out his notebook and wrote his name, serial number, and address. "Even if I'm transferred, you'll be able to trace me through my serial number."

"All right!" said Butsko. *"The vacation is over! Let's move it out!"*

The men kissed their women one last time, then moved away slowly and joined Butsko on the side of the car closest to the gate. They looked at the women and smiled sadly, while Longtree wished he had somebody to say good-bye to also.

"C'mon," Butsko said. "Let's not make this any harder than it is already."

The men shuffled toward the main gate, where two MPs with chrome helmets and white gloves were standing guard, checking orders. The women watched them go, their eyes filled with tears, as the men took out their orders and showed them to the MPs. The soldiers passed through the gates and looked back, waving at the women. Then the soldiers turned and walked away, heading back to the war.

ELEVEN . . .

Their C-47 touched down at Henderson Field on Guadalcanal after dark. Colonel Stockton wasn't on the plane with them. The plane taxied and stopped near the hangars, where so many Japanese bombs and artillery shells had landed that autumn. The stairs were moved next to the plane and the soldiers descended them, sick at heart to be back on that godforsaken island.

It even smelled different from Hawaii. There were no bright neon lights, no movie theaters, no pretty girls walking around in thin cotton dresses. It was just grim old Guadalcanal, with military discipline, training, fatigue duty, KP, and all the chickenshit that Army officers, with nothing better to do, dreamed up.

Glumly they made their way across the field and headed for the Eighty-first Division area and then to the Twenty-third Regiment, not saying anything, thinking about the women they had left behind. They felt desolate and alone, for love is the rarest commodity on a military installation. They heard the clank of military equipment being moved around, and the engines of jeeps and deuce-and-a-half trucks. Sergeants and officers shouted at men, and men's voices could be heard coming from pup tents, singing to the accompaniment of guitars about the blue hills of Kentucky or the Mississippi Delta, the plains of Iowa or Forty-second Street.

The men from the recon platoon were heartsick and almost nauseous by the time they reached the headquarters of the Twenty-third Regiment.

"You men wait here," Butsko said. "I'll go in and report."

Butsko looked at his watch: it was eight o'clock in the evening. He climbed the steps to the small wooden building and pushed open the screen door. Seated behind the desk was Lieutenant McClintock from Headquarters Company, the officer of the day.

"I'm back from furlough with three of my men," Butsko said. "Here's our orders." He threw them on the desk.

McClintock looked them over. "Everything looks okay to me. I've got a note here from Sergeant Major Ramsay that says you're supposed to report to the old man first thing in the morning."

"He's back already?" Butsko asked.

"No, but we expect him tomorrow. And tell your men they're confined to the company area until further notice."

"How come?"

"The old man's orders. Ask him."

"He must really be pissed at us."

"I reckon that's so," McClintock said.

Butsko left the office and returned to his men, who were standing around in the darkness, smoking cigarettes.

"Nobody leaves the company area until further notice," Butsko told them. "Fall out."

"How come we can't leave the company area?" Frankie asked.

"The old man is pissed at us, so watch your step."

Butsko trudged off, heading toward his pup tent, and the other three looked at each other. They shrugged and followed Butsko into the jungle.

After morning chow Butsko returned to Colonel Stockton's headquarters and saw his old buddy, Sergeant Major Ramsay, seated behind his desk against the right wall.

"Look who's back," said Ramsay with no enthusiasm in his voice.

"The old man in yet?" Butsko asked.

"Not yet. Have a seat. He should be here before long."

Butsko sat down and took out a cigarette. He wore green fatigues and combat boots, with his old yardbird hat on his lap. His six days in Honolulu seemed like a dream to him already.

"Hey, Ramsay," said Butsko, "where's the old man?"

"He's on his way back from Hawaii."

"I have the feeling that he's mad at me."

Ramsay looked up at Butsko from the morning's messages on his desk. "Whatever gives you that idea?" he asked, deadpan.

"He's really is, huh?"

"You'd better believe it."

"What's he gonna do?"

"I don't know, but you'd better get ready for the worst. You've made a lot of trouble for him, whether you know it or not."

"What kind of trouble?"

"I think he should be the one to tell you that."

"C'mon, Ramsay, don't be such a prick."

"All I got to say is that you and those baboons you went on furlough with are in a whole world of trouble in this regiment. If I was you, I wouldn't count on wearing those stripes much longer."

Butsko looked down at the master sergeant's stripes on his arms. So the old man was going to bust him. Well, he'd been busted before. It was no big thing. He'd just stand with the rest of the men in the formations and not have to make any more decisions. Let somebody else make the decisions. It was all bullshit no matter how you looked at it.

The sun rose in the sky and the day became hotter. Officers and enlisted men arrived at the orderly room and left off papers or picked them up. Ramsay's clerk, Pfc. Levinson, pounded his typewriter behind the desk on the other side of the room. Butsko chain-smoked cigarettes and thought about Dolly. He wondered what she was doing just then. Probably still in bed, because Dolly always liked to sleep late, entwined in her flimsy nightgowns and the expensive perfumes that she wore.

Where did she get the money to buy all those perfumes? How did she live so well without having a job? The allotment she got from him wasn't that much, so who was giving her the dough? Butsko became angry and jealous again. If only she was the kind of woman who was quiet and did what she was told. Instead she gave him something to worry about every time he thought about her. *That goddamn Dolly. I wish I could forget her.*

At ten o'clock in the morning Colonel Stockton entered the orderly room, attired in a starched tan Class A uniform, tailored to his long, lean body. He looked at Butsko; there were no smiles, no friendly words of greeting as in days gone by when Butsko used to visit Colonel Stockton and they'd shoot the shit for hours in his office. Colonel Stockton looked coldly, even angrily, at Butsko, then snapped his eyes away and turned to Sergeant Major Ramsay, who gave him a stack of important papers that had come in that morning.

Without a word Colonel Stockton took them into his office and closed the door. Butsko lit another cigarette, his hands shaking. He was afraid because he knew that Colonel Stockton had the power and authority to do just about anything with him that he wanted.

Butsko waited to be called into Colonel Stockton's office, and the time passed slowly. He knew what Colonel Stockton was doing now. Colonel Stockton was making him wait and worry, imagining all the punishment that could be inflicted. But Butsko knew that Colonel Stockton wouldn't put him in the stockade or anything like that. Colonel Stockton needed him for the upcoming campaign on New Georgia.

Butsko continued to chain-smoke, and every five or ten minutes he looked at his watch. The waiting was driving him nuts. His furlough in Honolulu had been a disaster. He'd spent most of it in the Honolulu jail, and he'd never even had time to get laid or sleep in a real bed. All his nights had been spent on that slab of wood in his jail cell. All because of Dolly. That goddamned Dolly.

Sergeant Major Ramsay's phone rang. Ramsay picked up the receiver and listened for a few moments, then hung up. He looked at Butsko and said: "You can go in now."

Butsko felt as if he'd just been given the death sentence.

He stubbed out his cigarette, stood, and smoothed the front of his uniform. Then he walked slowly toward the door of Colonel Stockton's office. He thought it would be easier for him if he didn't know Colonel Stockton so well, because he could put up with any kind of shit from someone he didn't know. But he and Colonel Stockton had been friends, and now Colonel Stockton was mad at him.

He opened the door and entered Colonel Stockton's office. Colonel Stockton sat behind his desk, reading correspondence, puffing his pipe, treating Butsko as if he weren't there. Butsko marched to the desk and saluted sharply.

"Master Sergeant John Butsko reporting, sir!"

Colonel Stockton continued reading the correspondence in his hands while Butsko stood at attention, his forehead covered with a slick of perspiration and his armpits getting itchy. Colonel Stockton was treating him as if his presence weren't even worth acknowledging. Butsko stood stiffly, looking down at the silver hair parted on the side and combed neatly on Colonel Stockton's head. He could imagine the little wheels turning inside that head, dreaming up horrors for Sergeant Butsko.

Finally Colonel Stockton looked up, and his blue eyes were as cold as chips of ice. He scrutinized Butsko as if he were inspecting a side of beef that was rotten and infested with maggots. Then Colonel Stockton stood and gazed into Butsko's eyes. Butsko could feel Colonel Stockton's anger stabbing into his brain. The expression in Colonel Stockton's eyes was more withering than any machine-gun fire he'd ever faced, and Butsko felt like collapsing onto the floor.

"You let me down," Colonel Stockton said in a deadly tone.

"I'm sorry, sir. I . . ."

Colonel Stockton interrupted him. "I trusted you and you let me down. I got you a furlough when nobody in this division was getting furloughs and you paid me back by ruining my career."

"Ruining your career?" Butsko asked. "What do you mean?"

"I'll ask the questions here, and you'll answer them! Otherwise keep your mouth shut!"

"Yes, sir."

"Ever since I organized the recon platoon and put you in charge, I've been criticized by everybody. They told me I should put an officer in charge of the recon platoon. They told me that the recon platoon consisted mainly of a bunch of criminals and misfits who'd be in jail in civilian life, but I always stuck up for you and said you were good soldiers, the best in the regiment, and that an officer would only cramp your style. Now you've embarrassed me in this regiment, in this division, and throughout the entire Pacific Theater. I let four of you go on furlough, and within twenty-four hours one of you was in jail for manslaughter, and another, a master sergeant who had been my friend, was in jail for aggravated assault. Within only twenty-four hours. And it's been all over the newspapers. Even General MacArthur read about it in Australia. And it all reflects on me. It makes me look bad. You've given my career a blow from which it may never recover."

"I'm sorry, sir," Butsko said, feeling awful. "I didn't mean . . ."

"Shut up!"

"Yes, sir."

Colonel Stockton sat back in his chair and folded his hands on his desk, looking up at Butsko. "You've disgraced yourself, you've disgraced your regiment, and you've disgraced me. As of today you're a private again. Corporal Bannon is a private again too. And Sergeant Cameron will be the new platoon sergeant of the recon platoon until further notice. An officer will be placed in charge of the recon platoon within twenty-four hours. Any questions?"

Butsko still was standing at attention. "Sir, I'd like to say something."

"Keep your mouth shut if you don't have a question!"

"Yes, sir."

Colonel Stockton pinched his lips together and narrowed his eyes at Butsko. "I've been forced to admit that I've been wrong about you all along. I thought you were a man, but instead you're an animal, just as everyone has been telling me all along. I've protected you and the other men in the recon platoon ever since it was formed, but now I'm withdrawing my protection. You've been good soldiers sometimes, but what you did in Hololulu is unforgivable. Now you're going to have to toe the mark just like everyone else around here. You'll be just another bunch of soldiers from now on, except I'm going to be tougher on you than the others. I want you to return to your platoon area, and the first thing I want you to do is take those sergeant's stripes off all your uniforms. From now on you'll take your orders from Sergeant Cameron and the officer who is placed in charge of the recon platoon. Any questions?"

"No, sir."

"You're dismissed."

Private Butsko raised his hand to his forehead and saluted, his face expressionless and his eyes clear. He did an about-face, marched to the door, and left the office.

The door closed, and Colonel Stockton relaxed behind his desk. He'd reamed Butsko out and busted him and didn't feel any remorse whatever, because he believed that Butsko had cost him his star. Ever since he'd been a little boy he'd wanted to be a general, and he'd had that star within his grasp, but Butsko had caused him to be shunted aside, and the star had been awarded to somebody else.

That's what happens when you're lenient with enlisted men, Colonel Stockton thought. *That's why officers are told never to become friendly with enlisted men. You can't keep the separation, otherwise they lose respect for you and do as they please. You can't keep them in line unless you keep them scared. What a fool I've been, to make a bunch of men like Butsko and his recon platoon into something special. I'll never do it again.*

Frowning, Colonel Stockton picked up a new directive from General MacArthur's headquarters in Brisbane and held it up to the light so that he could read it.

"Here he comes!" shouted Private Nutsy Gafooley, running through the jungle.

The recon platoon was gathered around their little corner of the regiment, waiting for Butsko to return. Nutsy had been posted as lookout outside Colonel Stockton's headquarters and now he was returning with his notification, his cheeks flushed with exertion and his eyes popping out. He was one of the smallest, skinniest men in the platoon, and had been hobo before the draft caught up with him.

The men from the recon platoon stood up and crowded around the path through which Butsko would come. They wore green fatigues and combat boots and had worried expressions on their faces, because they knew something terrible had happened to Butsko.

Butsko appeared on the trail, his yardbird hat low over his

eyes and high on the back of his head. He looked down at the ground and his shoulders were hunched, as if he didn't have the strength to stand straight. The muscles in his battered face sagged and he looked utterly defeated.

They swarmed around him as he entered the clearing.

"What happened, Sarge?" Nutsy asked, jumped up and down, trying to see over the heads and shoulders of the other men.

"I'm not your sarge anymore," Butsko replied. "I'm a private again, and so's Bannon. Sergeant Cameron is the new platoon sergeant, and we're getting a new platoon leader." Butsko pursed his lips, turned his head to the side, and spat at the ground. "That's about it."

Everyone was stunned. They knew Butsko would get chewed out, but they didn't think Colonel Stockton would bust him down. They followed Butsko like sleepwalkers as he trudged to his little pup tent, crawled inside, and closed the flap. A few minutes later they saw curls of cigarette smoke rise from the opening where the shelter halves had been buttoned together, and shortly after that they heard the snip-snip of scissors as Butsko cut off his master sergeant's stripes.

All the men knew that from then on things were going to be very different in the recon platoon.

First Lieutenant Dale Appleton Breckenridge was six feet five inches tall and tipped the scales at 265 pounds. He had a pug nose and the skin of his face was lumpy and pitted, due to the extreme acne attacks he'd suffered in his youth. His sleeves were rolled up over his massive biceps and he wore a fatigue cap that resembled a baseball cap as he approached the headquarters of the Twenty-third Infantry Regiment. He dropped his cigarette into the red butt can affixed to the banister and climbed the stairs onto the veranda, opening the door and stepping into Sergeant Major Ramsay's orderly room.

"Lieutenant Breckenridge here to see Colonel Stockton," he said to Ramsay.

"I'll tell him you're here."

Lieutenant Breckenridge clasped his hands behind his back and looked around the orderly room, seeing orders and memoranda tacked to bulletin boards, the bookcase full of ARs, and Pfc. Levinson banging his typewriter. Lieutenant Breckenridge was a platoon leader in Company D, commanding the weapons platoon, and had just made first lieutenant. He was hoping to become the executive officer of a company, the next logical step up the military ladder for him, and he hoped Colonel Stockton had called him in to say he was being assigned those new duties.

Sergeant Major Ramsay spoke on the phone for a few moments, listened, and then hung up. "The colonel will see you now."

Lieutenant Breckenridge walked to the door of the colonel's office, his every step making the floorboards creak and the building shake slightly. He opened the door and walked into Colonel Stockton's office, saluting precisely.

"Lieutenant Breckenridge reporting, sir."

"Sit down, Lieutenant."

"Thank you, sir."

Lieutenant Breckenridge sat on the chair in front of the desk and crossed his legs, making himself comfortable. He was from an old Virginia family that traced its heritage back to the Revolutionary War, and they were quite wealthy, which gave Lieutenant Breckenridge a certain amount of social and economic self-assurance that other, less fortunate people didn't have. Colonel Stockton looked him over and concluded that Lieutenant Breckenridge had that indefinable military quality known as command presence, although he was an OCS graduate, a "ninety-day wonder." Colonel Stockton fingered through the papers in Lieutenant Breckenridge's personnel file, athough he knew a lot about Lieutenant Breckenridge already. Breckenridge had proven himself to be a tough, resourceful young officer during the fight for Guadalcanal. He'd been awarded a Silver Star and a Purple Heart. Although he looked like a big lazy oaf, he had evidently been able to inspire his men to do outstanding things.

"Well," said Colonel Stockton, smiling cordially like a father to a his son, "you've compiled quite a record since you've been in the Army, Lieutenant. You'll probably have a brilliant future ahead of you if you want to make the Army your career."

"I don't know," Lieutenant Breckenridge said in a slow, easy drawl, the kind of voice that suggested he never got upset about anything. "I try not to think too far ahead. I just take each day as it comes."

"Yes," said Colonel Stockton, "I imagine that's a good way

141

to look at it, but what would you like to do in the Army, since you're part of it now? What are your goals?"

"I'd like to be a company commander someday," Lieutenant Breckenridge replied, "but first I suppose I'll have to be an executive officer, so I guess that's my next step."

"Well," said Colonel Stockton, "if things work out for you, we might be able to pass that step and move you right into the command of a company, but first there's something I'd like you to do for me. Are you familiar with my recon platoon?"

"I'm not that familiar with them, but I've heard about them," Lieutenant Breckenridge said. "They're supposed to be a pretty wild bunch."

"They've gotten a little too wild," Colonel Stockton replied. "I've decided that they need a good officer to keep them in line. Do you think you can handle them?"

"I can handle anybody," Lieutenant Breckenridge said easily, without a trace of doubt in his voice.

"Do you want the job?"

"I don't know, sir. It seems like I'd just be doing more or less what I'm doing now. I told you that I'd like to be a company commander, and my next logical step before that would be to become executive officer."

Colonel Stockton leaned forward and looked into Lieutenant Breckenridge's eyes. "The man who can handle the recon platoon can just about write his own ticket in this regiment," he said. "If you run them right for six months and give them some of the old-fashioned military discipline that they need, you'll get the first company that becomes available, and that's a promise."

"But, sir," said Lieutenant Breckenridge, "there are a lot of officers in the regiment who have more time in grade than I do."

"Time in grade doesn't mean a shit in this Army," Colonel Stockton said bitterly, recalling how he'd lost his star to a man who had less time in grade than he. "I'll decide what the assignments are in this company, and this is a promise I'm making to you. Is that clear?"

"Yes, sir," Lieutenant Breckenridge thought for a few moments. He knew Colonel Stockton was a man of his word and he would fulfill his promise, but did Lieutenant Breckenridge want to take on the recon platoon? He knew their reputation, and the men in the regiment didn't call them the Rat Bastards for nothing. They were said to be a bunch of ex-convicts and killers whom Colonel Stockton had welded together into a crack fighting unit, but maybe they were becoming unstuck now that the battle for Guadalcanal was over.

"Well," said Colonel Stockton, "what do you say?"

"If you want me to do it, I'll do it, sir."

"You're sure?"

"Yes, sir."

"Good." Colonel Stockton rubbed his hands together. "What do you know about the recon platoon?"

"Not a hell of a lot. They're supposed to be a tough bunch of boys."

"They've done amazing things on Guadalcanal," Colonel Stockton said, "but their problem is sometimes they forget they're in the Army. It'll be your job to make them aware that they're in the Army and they have to follow orders. If they ever step out of line, you're the one who'll have to bring them back into line. Do you know who Master Sergeant Butsko is?"

"I've seen him around."

"What do you think of him?"

"He looks like a mean son of a bitch. Why can't he keep them in line?"

Colonel Stockton gritted his teeth together. *"Because he's as bad as they are!* You think you can handle him?"

"I can handle anybody," Lieutenant Breckenridge said again.

"You're going to have your hands full, Lieutenant. The men in the recon platoon aren't used to having an officer telling them what to do. In fact, they've been doing just fine without an officer until recently, when they went to Honolulu on furlough. I take it you know what I'm referring to?"

"Yes, sir. I read about it in the papers."

"There's no point in going into that any more, but anyway, the incident made it clear to me that the recon platoon is out of control and needs to be placed back in control. It won't be easy but I think you can do it. I think you should go to Personnel first and look over the records of the men in the recon platoon, and then in the morning you should take charge, and anything you want to do is okay with me—you don't have to check with me. How does that sound?"

"Sounds fine, sir."

"I thought you'd say that. The orders will be cut today and will be effective tomorrow. The recon platoon is all yours, and if you shape them up, you'll be a company commander in six months; but if they make a fool of you, you'll never be able to hold your head up in this regiment again. Understand?"

Lieutenant Breckenridge grinned, pulling back his thick lips and showing his long white teeth. "No bunch of Rat Bastards is going to make a fool out of me," he said with absolute self-confidence.

It was night on Guadalcanal, and the men from the recon platoon were gathering around in the darkness, drinking PX beer and smoking cigarettes while birds squawked in the trees and wild dogs in the distant jungle bayed at the moon.

"I've never seen him like this," Nutsy Gafooley said grimly, a bottle of beer in his hand. "I think he's gone over the edge."

Craig Delane, the rich guy from New York, nodded his head. "It's as if all the fight has gone out of him."

Corporal Gomez, the pachuco from Los Angeles, took a drag on his cigarette. "You don't think he's gonna blow his brains out, do you?"

Bannon shook his head. "Naw, he won't do that."

"I never thought he'd take it so hard," Frankie La Barbara said. "I mean, he's been busted before lots of times. What's one more?"

"Maybe," said Corporal Baines, "this is the straw that broke the camel's back."

"Naw," replied Bannon, "it ain't that. He just thinks that he's let Colonel Stockton down. They were buddies once."

"Yeah?" asked Private Slater, who was new to the recon platoon. "How can a sergeant and a colonel be buddies?"

"Don't ask me," Bannon said, "but they were."

"Sure they were," Frankie La Barbara agreed. "They used to have long bullshit sessions in Colonel Stockton's office. They even used to plan strategy together." Frankie shrugged. "Well, I've seen Butsko's old lady. No wonder he's half out of his mind. She's a real blockbuster dame."

"Yeah?" asked Nutsy. "Is she pretty?"

"She's a real hot-looking old broad," Frankie said. "I wouldn't mind throwing a fuck into her myself, but for Chrissakes don't tell Butsko that."

144

Morris Shilansky, the ex-bank robber from Boston, lay on his back and looked up at the stars. "I wonder what the new looie is gonna be like."

Frankie chuckled. "We'll make the son of a bitch wish he was never born."

"Don't be too sure about that," Bannon said. "I hear he's tough."

Frankie tapped the stock of his M 1. "Ain't nobody tougher than a bullet."

"You got your head up your ass again, Frankie," Bannon said. "All of us, including Butsko, will be in more trouble than ever if you shoot the looie."

Frankie shrugged. "Maybe you're right."

"I know what we gotta do," said Pfc. Shaw, who had been a professional heavyweight boxer before the war. "We gotta shape up and really soldier hard. That way we'll look good and Butsko'll look good, and maybe, when we get back into combat again, the looie will get shot and Butsko'll wind up in charge again. When the shit hits the fan, the colonel will know that only one man can run the recon platoon, and that's Butsko, whether the colonel likes it or not."

"Yeah," said Nutsy Gafooley, "but what if the new looie doesn't get shot?"

"Oh," replied Frankie La Barbara, "I think he'll get shot. Anything can happen in combat. They say the road to Tokyo is gonna be paved with dead looies."

"Jesus," Bannon said, "can you guys ever think of doing something without killing somebody."

"All I know," Frankie told him, "is that a good looie is a dead looie."

A few of the men grunted in assent. Longtree sat silently nearby and sharpened his bayonet. He saw a light go on for an instant in Butsko's tent and then go out again. Butsko was lighting another cigarette. What was he thinking about all alone in his tent? What was he doing? Was he going nuts? Longtree shook his head sadly. It was bad for everybody when a great warrior like Butsko lost his power. *There will be many bad days ahead for the recon platoon,* Longtree thought unhappily.

TWELVE . . .

The next morning after chow the recon platoon was policing their bivouac area, tightening the guy lines of their tents, and performing all the other tasks that needed to be done before beginning the day of training.

Nutsy Gafooley was hammering in one of his tent pegs, when suddenly the day grew dark all around him. Somebody was blocking the sun, and he turned around to see a hulking man standing behind him like a giant.

"What's your name, soldier?"

"Who wants to know?" asked Nutsy Gafooley.

A massive hand descended from heaven and landed on Nutsy's neck, grabbing his collar and nearly knocking him unconscious. The hand pulled Nutsy to his feet and turned him around, so Nutsy could see the shiny silver lieutenant's bars on his collar and hat.

"I said what's your name, soldier?" Lieutenant Breckenridge asked again, holding Nutsy suspended in the air.

"Private Marion Gafooley, recon platoon, Twenty-third Regiment, sir!"

"Find Sergeant Cameron and tell him I want to see him on the double."

"Yes, sir."

Lieutenant Breckenridge dropped Nutsy, who hit the ground running, heading for the place where he'd last seen Sergeant Cameron. Lieutenant Breckenridge stood with his arms dangling at his sides and let his eyes rove over the platoon area, which looked neat and orderly, not the dump he'd expected to find. Evidently the recon platoon knew how to soldier. All they needed was some leadership, and that he intended to provide.

Just as he looked over the men, they quickly became aware of his presence and examined him from a safe distance.

"Big son of a bitch, ain't he?" Bannon said to Frankie La Barbara.

"Looks pretty mean too," Frankie replied.

"He's even bigger than Shaw."

"I think he's bigger than Shaw, me, and you put together."

Nutsy found Sergeant Cameron and brought him to Lieutenant Breckenridge. Cameron was a pleasant young man who wasn't outstanding in any way but had never done anything blatantly wrong and therefore had become the platoon sergeant by default. He marched up to Lieutenant Breckenridge and saluted.

"Sergeant Cameron reporting, sir."

Lieutenant Breckenridge returned the salute. "I'm your new platoon leader. My name is Breckenridge—Lieutenant Dale Breckenridge. Form up your platoon in that clearing over there so I can talk with them."

"Yes, sir!"

Sergeant Cameron saluted and dashed off, hollering orders. The men broke off their police calls and work on the tents, double-timing toward the clearing and forming four squad ranks. Butsko crawled out of his tent and stood up, and his eyes fell on the huge lieutenant on the other side of the clearing. Breckenridge appeared to be looking in his direction.

So that's him, Butsko thought. *Well, well, well.*

Butsko took his position in the First Squad, which was Bannon's former squad, now led by Pfc. Longtree. The men dressed right and covered down. They stood at attention as Lieutenant Breckenridge sauntered to the front of the formation and accepted the salute of Sergeant Cameron.

"At ease!" shouted Lieutenant Breckenridge.

The men kicked out their left legs and clasped their hands

148

behind their backs, then relaxed into the at-ease position. Lieutenant Breckenridge's eyes swept back and forth over them; he looked immense in comparison to Sergeant Cameron, who was only five feet ten inches tall.

"I guess you men know who I am," the big officer said, "but in case you don't, I'm Lieutenant Dale Breckenridge, your new platoon leader." He paused to let that sink in. The men's faces were immobile. "Now I've heard that you're a pretty tough bunch and I'm glad to know that, because I wouldn't want to command a platoon of sissies and cowards. You're also supposed to be hard to handle, but that's okay with me, because the best soldiers are always a little hard to handle. I'm the first officer the recon platoon has ever had, and you probably don't like the idea of having me around, but I've been assigned to you and we both have to make the best of things. If you want to make things hard for me, I'll make things hard for you. Make them easy for me, and I'll make them easy for you. You can have it any way you want it. I'd rather take things easy, but I don't mind it when things get tough. When the going gets tough, the tough get going. That's the way I see it." He paused. "In a few weeks more or less we're going to New Georgia, and we're going to start training intensively starting tomorrow. It won't be easy, but I won't ask you to do anything I wouldn't do myself. Any man who fucks off will be on my shit list. The man who does what he's told will get along just fine; I'll back him up one hundred percent in anything he does. But the man who gets on my shit list will wish he was dead. Any questions so far?"

Nobody said anything. The recon platoon stood as still as forty statues lined up in the jungle, and nobody batted an eyelash.

"Good," said Lieutenant Breckenridge. "Now, there's one last thing: If anybody has any legitimate complaint, I'm always available. I don't want you to waste my time with every silly problem that comes along, but if anything serious comes up, let me know and I'll do what I can. We're all in this war together, and if we stick together and help each other, we stand a chance of getting home in one piece someday. I'm not a career officer, gentlemen. I want to go home too. Any questions?"

Nobody said anything.

"Okay," said Lieutenant Breckenridge. "I want Private Butsko to report to me after this formation is dismissed. Platoon—atten-hut! *Fall out!*"

The platoon formation broke apart as Butsko walked forward toward Lieutenant Breckenridge. The others watched Butsko's trajectory, expecting a major confrontation and explosion. They knew Breckenridge wanted to put Butsko in his place, otherwise he wouldn't have called Butsko forward; and they knew Butsko definitely would not let himself be put in any place.

Butsko advanced and threw a snappy salute. "Private Butsko reporting, sir!" he said loudly, his shirt sleeves showing the discoloration where his master's sergeant's stripes had been.

Lieutenant Breckenridge measured him with his eyes, noticing the huge broad shoulders, expanse of chest, battered nose, and scarred face. Butsko reminded him of a bulldog who'd been in too many fights.

"Let's sit down someplace and have a talk." Breckenridge said. "You know this area better than I do. Where's a good spot?"

"Right over this way, sir."

"Lead the way."

Butsko veered off into the jungle, and Lieutenant Breckenridge walked at his side. Neither of them said a word, but Butsko couldn't help being aware of how much bigger Breckenridge was than he; it was an usual experience, because usually he was bigger than most of the men he met. Breckenridge looked like he was all muscle, with a cockiness that indicated he wasn't afraid to use what he had. Lieutenant Breckenridge would be nobody to fuck with, that was for sure. That must be why the colonel had assigned him to take over the recon platoon, Butsko figured.

They walked through the jungle and came to a small clearing eight feet in diameter, away from all the tents and the latrine. "This okay?" Butsko asked.

"It's fine. Have a seat."

Both dropped down on the grass and fallen leaves. Mosquitoes and other insects buzzed around their heads, and the odor of decaying vegetation filled their nostrils.

Lieutenant Breckenridge took out a pack of Camels and held it to Butsko. "Cigarette?"

"Thanks," said Butsko, taking one.

Lieutenant Breckenridge took a cigarette for himself and lit both with his Zippo, blowing smoke into the air.

"I guess you're not too happy about me being here," Lieutenant Breckenridge said, "right?"

Butsko shrugged. "It don't mean a fuck to me one way or another."

"I don't believe that. You don't want an officer running this platoon any more than you want another nose."

"Believe what you wanna believe, sir."

Lieutenant Breckenridge smiled. "You don't resent me being here just a little bit?"

"Maybe a little bit," Butsko admitted. "But not much."

"I've been looking at your records," Lieutenant Breckenridge said, "and you've had quite a military career. I guess I have to admit that you have more military experience than I do. I know all about you, and maybe it's only fair that I tell you something about me, so that we understand each other. You may be a private right now, but you and I both know that you're still the most powerful man in this platoon, and both of us have to face that, right?"

"Maybe."

"You're being coy, Private Butsko."

"You're talking some strange shit, Lieutenant Breckenridge."

"Maybe I am, but I'm gonna keep on talking it." Lieutenant Breckenridge spit into the grass and leaves. "I wanna get one thing straight with you. I'm only in this Army for the duration, and then I'm getting out. I was drafted into the Army—I didn't enlist—and I became an officer because I didn't want to put up with the crap that enlisted men have to put up with. I have no real ambitions in the Army except that I want to get out alive, and I'd like to be a company commander because I like to have as much control over my life as I can. Do you follow me so far?"

Butsko grunted.

"You're a career soldier," Lieutenant Breckenridge said, "and from what I know about you, you're a good soldier. You've made this recon platoon into an outfit that's talked about all over this island, but you have a problem: You can't deal with civilian life. Most of your problems have been off post, except for the time you punched an officer at Fort Sill and broke his jaw. You tend to be insubordinate at times, which gets you into trouble. But none of that matters to me. I don't care how crazy you are. All I know is that you're the unofficial platoon sergeant of the recon platoon. Everybody knows that and so do I. So do you. So let's start from there."

"You're wrong," Butsko said. "I'm just a private in the ranks and that's all I wanna be."

"Bullshit. You can fool yourself, but you can't fool me. But all that's beside the point. My concern is me. You can make my job tough or you can make it easy. You can work with me or you can work against me. If you decide to work against me, you'll find out that you can't push me around like some of the other young lieutenants. The colonel assigned me here, which means that I have a certain amount of power, and I'm not afraid to use power. If you make my life difficult, I'll make your life difficult. You help me and I'll help you. We're going to New Georgia pretty soon, and if you're the man I think you are, and the soldier I think you are, I'll make sure you'll have all your stripes back pretty soon. But if you want to be foolish, New Georgia just might become your graveyard. Get my drift?"

"Yeah," said Butsko, "but you're wrong about one thing: I don't want my stripes back. I just wanna be an ordinary soldier in the ranks, without any responsiblity and headaches. You can have the responsibility and headaches. Fuck those stripes."

Lieutenant Breckenridge chuckled. "I wonder if you're bullshitting me or bullshitting yourself."

"I'm telling the truth."

"Then you're bullshitting yourself, because you're a born leader and you know it. You'll always rise to the top. You'll get bored in the ranks because you know that you can do things better than Sergeant Cameron and even better than me. You'll want to take over and you should take over. This is your platoon. I don't want it. I want a company, and the colonel told me I can have it if I run this platoon smoothly for a while. So you can have this platoon back if you play your cards right. We can both get what we want if we cooperate. How do you feel about that?"

"Well," said Butsko, looking Lieutenant Breckenridge in the eye. "I'm a soldier. I don't know nothing else except soldiering, and a soldier follows orders and does his duty. That's the way it's gonna be between you and me. I'm gonna follow orders and do my duty, because that's all I know. If I get my stripes and this platoon back, I guess that wouldn't bother me too much. If I don't, that's okay by me too. I can take it either way. That's what I'm gonna do."

"That's good enough for me," Lieutenant Breckenridge said.

"There's one more thing," Butsko replied. "I'm always looking out for myself and my friends. If somebody tries to get us into trouble, I'm gonna step in. I'm telling you that to your face right now, so you'll know in advance."

"I'll listen to your advice anytime, Butsko, and in fact I'll welcome it. We'll have no problems there." He held out his hand. "Let's shake on it."

"I don't shake hands with officers," Butsko said.

Lieutenant Breckenridge withdrew his hand but didn't seem bothered. "Have it your own way. I don't have anything more to say. What about you?"

"Just one thing," Butsko smirked. "You and me can make whatever deals we wanna make and plan whatever we wanna plan, but when we land on New Georgia, that artillery shell with our name on it might land on us in the first hour, so it all doesn't make a shit anyway."

"You're right," Lieutenant Breckenridge agreed, "but it might not land on us, and if it doesn't, it's good to know where everything stands."

"Okay," Butsko said. "That makes sense."

"End of meeting," Lieutenant Breckenridge said.

Both men stood. Butsko saluted Lieutenant Breckenridge, who returned the salute. Butsko turned around and walked away, and Lieutenant Breckenridge puffed his cigarette and watched him go, proud of the way he'd handled him, because Lieutenant Breckenridge was a little intimidated by Butsko, who was older than he was and had seen a lot more war. Butsko had even survived the Bataan Death March.

Well, he's not completely crazy, Lieutenant Breckenridge thought. *If that bomb doesn't land on us on New Georgia, he and I will probably come out of this mess okay.*

Butsko returned to the platoon area and saw the men gath-

153

ered around, looking expectantly at him, because they thought a big blow-out had taken place between him and Lieutenant Breckenridge.

"Hey, Sarge," said Frankie La Barbara. "What happened?"

"Nothing happened," Butsko said, heading back to his tent.

"Whataya mean, nothing happened? Something hadda happen."

Butsko didn't reply; he just kept walking toward his tent. The entire platoon followed him like little children following the Pied Piper of Hamelin, but Butsko didn't acknowledge their presence.

Frankie caught up with Butsko and turned to him. "Hèy, Sarge, we've been talking and we figured out a way to fix that lieutenant's wagon."

Butsko stopped and looked at Frankie. "What are you talking about?"

The other men crowded around Butsko. Frankie grinned and held out his hands with the palms out. "We'll just keep fucking up until this looie looks so bad they'll have to transfer him out."

An expression of disgust came over Butsko's face. "So what good'll that do, you dumb fuck? They'll just send another officer over here. And besides, you're not gonna push this guy around much. You push him and he'll push back. He's as tough as any man here, and tougher than most of you. Not only that, he's the boss and you're gonna do what he says." Butsko pointed at Frankie. "Get it?"

"What for?"

"Because we're soldiers and we're gonna do what we're told. Any man who doesn't do his duty will have to answer to me. Got it?"

"What if he's no good?" Bannon asked.

"If he's no good, we'll put a bullet in his head," Butsko said matter-of-factly, "but I think he'll be all right. He knows the score. He's not out to break anybody's balls. I'm the guy who likes to break balls, remember?"

They all nodded, because they remembered the things Butsko had done to them over the past several months.

"We're gonna be the best soldiers we can be," Butsko said. "That's the only way we'll get off Colonel Stockton's shit list. Do you understand what I'm saying?"

The men nodded.

"Make sure you remember it," Butsko said. "As you were!"

Butsko turned and walked away. The men looked at each other, shrugged, and dispersed into small groups, buzzing and whispering, speculating about their future, tossing off notions that soon would become rumors and then facts all of them would eventually believe.

THIRTEEN . . .

The invasion of New Georgia, code-named Operation TOENAILS, was launched during the latter part of June, with a preliminary landing on the nearby island of Rendova, to cut off Japanese communications with Rabaul. Then the main landings took place at Segi Point, Wickham Anchorage, Viru Harbor, Rice Anchorage, and the town of Zanana, the latter near the principal military objective on New Georgia, the Japanese airfield on Munda Point.

Ground forces were under the command of Major General John H. Hester and consisted initially of the heavily reinforced Forty-third Infantry Division, the Ninth Marine Defense Battalion, the First Marine Raider Regiment minus two battalions, and elements of the First Commando of Fiji Guerillas.

Among the units held in reserve was the Eighty-first Division on Guadalcanal, which trained day and night in amphibious landings, jungle fighting, speed marches, and maneuvers of all types, large scale and small scale, waiting for orders to move to New Georgia and bail out whoever was in trouble.

The trouble began soon after the landings, when the inexperienced Forty-third Infantry Division became bogged down. The Japanese forces on New Georgia, commanded by the brilliant and resourceful Major General Noboru Sasaki, fought back ferociously, holding the GIs to a standstill during the day and attacking them relentlessly at night.

The constant round-the-clock combat and the inexperience of the Forty-third Division's officers and men resulted in a stalled offensive. American casualties mounted to horrifying levels, and for the first time in the history of the US Army a large number of casualties were diagnosed as suffering from war neuroses. About 1,500 such cases were reported between the thirtieth of June and the thirty-first of July.

The Army responded by sending in Colonel Franklin T. Hallam, surgeon of the XIV Corps, when the mental breakdowns were at their height. After an investigation he concluded that *war neuroses* was a "misnomer in most instances," because men who were physically exhausted "were erroneously directed or gravitated through medical channels along with the true psychoneurotics and those suffering with the temporary medical disturbance called war neuroses." He further noted that war neuroses occurred most frequently in units with poor leadership.

The military situation on New Georgia deteriorated steadily for the Americans, and on the sixteenth of July, General Hester was relieved of command. He was replaced by Major General Oscar W. Griswold, commanding officer of the XIV Corps and the Guadalcanal Island Base.

It was General Griswold's first experience in commanding a corps in combat, and upon arrival on New Georgia he concluded that the airfield at Munda Point couldn't be taken without massive reinforcements. He also saw the necessity of reorganizing his occupation force for a more effective response to the Japanese counterattacks.

Griswold decided that pressure had to be kept on the Japanese through a series of local attacks with limited objectives, chiefly to secure more advantageous ground for a major offensive.

Then he sent for his backup forces on Guadalcanal.

On July 18, General Clyde Hawkins, the commanding officer of the Eighty-first Division on Guadalcanal, received his orders. The division was to board ships on July 20 and depart for New Georgia. He passed along the order to all his commands, telling them where they'd fight and what their missions would be.

Colonel Stockton received his orders shortly before noon. The Twenty-third would be landed near Zanana to relieve the 169th Infantry Regiment, which had been on New Georgia since the first landings and had been chewed to shreds by General Sasaki's fanatical soldiers. The Twenty-third's mission would be to press forward and capture Munda Point, in concert with other units.

Colonel Stockton called for a meeting of his battalion commanders, but the word was already going out on the grapevine, transmitted by Sergeant Major Ramsay to his friends, and Pfc. Levinson to his friends, and friends told friends, and the only people who didn't find out early were the battalion commanders and other top-ranking brass, who would get the word at Colonel Stockton's meeting.

FOURTEEN . . .

The Twenty-third Infantry Regiment landed near the town of Zanana on the night of July 20 and waded ashore from their landing ships and barges with no Japanese opposition. Colonel Stockton went ashore with the first wave and set up his headquarters and communications on the beach so that he could ride herd on his regiment and make sure they moved swiftly. He wore combat fatigues and his steel helmet, and strapped to his waist was his Army-issue Colt .45, loaded and ready for action.

There wouldn't be much action until the Twenty-third relieved the 169th in the jungle near Munda Point, but Colonel Stockton wanted to set the tone for the days ahead. He wanted his men to see him on the beach, armed to the teeth and ready to fight, a real combat commander, who was *leading* them instead of following at a safe distance.

He knew that most battles were won by the army with the highest morale, all other factors being equal, and he knew that an officer had to inspire his men by setting the proper example. Whip them into a frenzy and send them into battle: That was his motto. Scare them, prod them, scream at them, praise them and exalt them if you had to, but get them moving at all costs.

The soldiers who stayed where they were and dug in were the surest candidates for the graveyard. The soldiers who attacked hard and kicked ass were the ones who survived and won glory for themselves and their regiments.

After getting set up, Colonel Stockton placed his executive officer in charge of his headquarters and then went down to the beach to supervise the unloading of the landing craft and to show himself to his men, so that they'd know he was there just like they were, breaking his hump too.

The recon platoon arrived in the first wave and took positions in the jungle, awaiting further orders. They didn't dig in because they didn't intend to stay long, but they set up a defense perimeter so they'd be prepared for Japanese infiltrators.

It was weird to be back in a combat zone, and all the veterans felt the old fear returning, sharpening their senses and enlivening their minds. They knew the Japs weren't far away and that a big push was being planned. The Japs were dug in and well camouflaged around the airfield at Munda Point; it wouldn't be easy to wipe them out. According to all reports, they were fighting to the last man, the way they did on Guadalcanal.

Butsko rested on one knee behind a bush, carrying a flamethrower on his back. It weighed seventy pounds and didn't feel heavy yet, but he knew it would drag down his shoulders and cause him great pain after a few hours of walking through the jungle. Also, flamethrower operators had a short life span, because they had to expose the upper part of their torso to enemy fire in order to operate the equipment effectively.

Butsko wanted to smoke a cigarette, but there was no smoking at night in combat zones. All his old war-dog instincts were coming back, and he remembered what Lieutenant Breckenridge had told him about being a born leader. Now that the recon platoon was on New Georgia, Butsko felt an urge to take over and lead the men. He knew he could lead them better than Sergeant Cameron and even better than Lieutenant Breckenridge himself, because although Breckenridge was a good officer, he simply didn't have the experience Butsko had. The good thing about Lieutenant Breckenridge was that he knew it and made no bones about it. Many times during maneuvers on Guadalcanal Lieutenant Breckenridge had called Butsko aside and asked him his advice on how to proceed. Everybody was

162

aware of this, and even Sergeant Cameron accepted it. Butsko had become the real but unofficial platoon sergeant of the recon platoon, with everything being done in a roundabout way so that visitors from other units and snoopy officers from Headquarters wouldn't suspect anything unusual. Officially Butsko was a private with a flamethrower on his back, the guy who'd been busted because he'd gotten on the wrong side of Colonel Stockton.

Meanwhile, in the First Squad, Bannon had become the real but unofficial squad leader, with Longtree as his assistant, more or less, the way things were before the disastrous furlough in Honolulu.

In practice, the recon platoon was just the way it had always been, only now they had Lieutenant Breckenridge to run inference between them and Colonel Stockton's headquarters.

It wasn't a bad deal at all.

At one o'clock in the morning, most of the First Battalion was ashore and organized company by company and platoon by platoon, ready to move out. Colonel Stockton ordered the First Battalion forward to secure the left flank of the 169th Regiment's line, while the recon platoon would locate the 169th headquarters and conduct a quick reconnaissance of the area so that Colonel Stockton could move his own headquarters up as soon as possible. The rest of the regiment would follow in battalion echelons as soon as they were landed.

The recon platoon followed the First Battalion into the jungle, heading toward the 169th's line. Lieutenant Breckenridge marched at the head of the recon platoon. At his side was Nutsy Gafooley, his runner, carrying a walkie-talkie and the platoon bazooka. The rest of the men followed in a column of twos on a road plowed through the jungle by the Corps of Engineers.

In the distance directly in front of them, the men from the recon platoon heard sporadic gunfire and shelling, the old familiar sounds of night in a combat zone. They knew that Japs loved to fight at night, slipping through the jungle, slitting the throats of sleeping GIs, blowing up ammo dumps and food supplies, but you could stop them if you stayed alert and followed certain basic procedures like laying concertina wire in front of your position and festooning it with tin cans that would

163

rattle whenever a Jap tried to sneak through. You had to post guards and make sure they stood awake. And no one could fire wildly into the night. You had to get used to killing Japs with your Kabar knife, hand to hand.

All the old emotions and reflexes came back as the soldiers scoured the bushes and trees, looking for snipers, because there was always the possibility that Japs were close by. The GIs were ready to drop onto their bellies in an instant and start fighting. Their weapons were locked and loaded. They were ready to roll. And they wondered what would happen when the big push came, who would live and who would die, and who would be shipped back to the States minus arms or legs, basket cases for the rest of their lives.

Bannon carried his full field pack and M 1 rifle, not feeling any fatigue yet, because he was in good condition due to the endless training on Guadalcanal prior to the landing. After the first mile it became clear to him that there was no danger in that part of the jungle, and his mind wandered back to Honolulu, to little Nettie, and he wondered if she was still a whore in the Curtis Hotel or if she'd kept her word and quit.

She seemed so far away, almost like a dream. How strange it was that an ordinary woman could become a dream of paradise to a man because of the war. When there was no war it was no problem having girl friends or getting married. Even jerks were able to have girl friends and get married. Women were all over the damn place. But in wartime there were no women around, and a soldier's most pressing reality was misery and probable death. His only relief came from women in the flesh or via fantasies.

Bannon missed Nettie, especially since he figured that she needed him. She was fragile and strange, and anything could happen to a woman like her. She needed somebody to look out for her, and he needed her passionate, devoted love. They were perfect for each other, except for one thing: He might be dead by this time tomorrow.

He looked ahead into the darkness toward the direction of Munda Point. Somewhere out there was a Jap who might kill him. The Jap was probably sleeping, or maybe jabbing his knife into the jugular vein of a sleeping GI, but Bannon knew he was there. Bannon wanted to kill the Jap before the Jap killed him.

164

"I'm gonna get you, you fucking Jap," Bannon mumbled, "so you'd better watch your ass."

"What was that?" Frankie La Barbara asked.

"Nothing," replied Bannon.

"I thought you said something."

"Not me."

"Oh."

Frankie let his thoughts return to Janie, the little nurse at Pearl Harbor with whom he'd had a continuous orgy when he wasn't at court with Butsko and Bannon. She was a meek, pale girl who you wouldn't think would be a sex degenerate, but all she wanted to do was fuck, and she had a smile that would melt an iceberg. She wouldn't even let you get out of bed so you could take a piss.

Frankie couldn't understand why politicians started wars when there were better things to do, like screwing women. The Japs must not like to fuck, he figured. If they liked to fuck, they wouldn't have started the goddamned war.

His hatred of Japs rose in his throat and made him cough. They were the ones who were keeping him from pretty girls like Janie, and he was going to make them pay for it. The more of them he killed, the quicker he'd be back in her bed and the beds of others, because Frankie wanted to fuck them all before he died. He knew it was a lofty ambition, but what else was there to do?

He just hoped he didn't die before he had the chance to screw the next one, and the next one, and the next one.

The First Battalion moved up on the line at five o'clock in the morning, relieving the men from the 169th Regiment on the left flank. The recon platoon veered in a northwesterly direction, heading for the 169th headquarters, as the new day dawned on the horizon.

They moved across the 169th's line, being challenged as they encountered each new unit, and in the foxholes they saw men with beards, their eyes sunken deep into their heads, their chests bony, their hands trembling. They looked at the men from the recon platoon with hatred, because the men in the recon platoon were clean and well fed, while the 169th had been fighting the Japs day and night for nearly four weeks.

" 'Bout time you got here," one said angrily.

"You guys don't know what you're in for," another called out.

It took an hour for the recon platoon to find the headquarters of the 169th, and Lieutenant Breckenridge reported to the commanding officer, telling him they were in the area and would remain until Colonel Stockton arrived.

The headquarters of the 169th was all packed up and ready to move out except for a few tents that had to be struck. They pulled back and the recon platoon scouted around while Lieutenant Breckenridge determined how the new camp would be set up. When he had all the information he needed, he radioed back to Colonel Stockton and told him all was ready for him to move his headquarters up.

Throughout the morning and afternoon, units of the 169th Regiment pulled back, to be replaced by the Twenty-third Regiment. The men from the 169th looked as if nearly every bit of life had been squeezed out of them, while the Twenty-third was clean and sharp, full of piss and vinegar, ready to attack the Japs and take Munda Point away from them.

By nightfall the 169th had gone and the Twenty-third was in place, dug in, wired, and ready for action. In his command post tent Colonel Stockton went over the plans for his attack on Munda Point. It was going to be a full frontal attack with no fancy stuff, and he expected the Japs to be knocked for a loop because they were tired and he was fresh.

With a little dash and a lot of plain old American fighting spirit, he hoped to capture Munda Point in a few days. He wanted to beat every other outfit to the prize so General MacArthur would take notice. Then, when stars were passed around next time, he might get his finally.

FIFTEEN . . .

The sea and aerial bombardment of the Japanese defensive network began at 0614 hours on July 25. Over five hundred thousand pounds of fragmentation and high-explosive bombs were dropped by the Army Air Corps, and 3,332 howitzer shells were fired by artillery batteries on the ground.

The GIs waited in their foxholes for the barrage to end, hearing the awful din and watching the clouds of black smoke rise into the air in the distance. They gripped their rifles and their guts tied into knots, because they knew they'd be going over the top when the barrage ended.

Ahead of them was the Jap army. They didn't know how many Japs were there, but they knew they were formidable, for the Japs had fought the Forty-third Division to a standstill and kicked their asses on numerous occasions. The ground shuddered underneath the GIs, and they were glad the bombs and shells weren't falling on them.

The tension built with every passing moment. Every GI knew that the regiment always suffered casualties whenever they attacked. In the past the casualties had sometimes reached fifty percent. That was one out of every two men, and each wondered if he'd be the one who'd stop the bullet or get blown into hamburger by a Jap mortar round. Visions of death in all its horrific forms passed through the soldiers' minds, and they thought of their loved ones back home and how they'd react when they found out that their GI Joe had been cut down by the Japs.

The recon platoon was strung out in the series of foxholes, waiting with the rest for the attack to begin. Butsko and Bannon were together, not talking, smoking cigarettes and looking over the rim of their foxhole at the jungle ahead. Butsko had the flamethrower strapped to his back and Bannon carried an M 1 rifle. They both wore steel pots, cartridge belts, bayonets, and medical pouches. The minutes ticked away, bringing them closer to the moment when they'd attack.

Twenty yards away Lieutenant Breckenridge knelt in his foxhole, peering ahead at the bombardment through his binoculars. Beside him, Nutsy Gafooley sat with his back against the wall of the foxhole, sucking a cigarette, his walkie talkie hanging from one shoulder and the platoon bazooka hanging from the other. Nutsy blinked his eyes rapidly and chewed his lips, anxious to get going. He was a high-strung person and couldn't bear waiting for anything.

Lieutenant Breckenridge wasn't high strung and in fact was rather low strung, but he felt the awful weight of responsibility on his shoulders, because deep down he was a sensitive man and knew he held the lives of his men in the palm of his hand. They would live or die according to his mistakes and shortcomings, or survive according to his strength and clarity of mind. All the pressure was on him, and he had a million things to worry about, including the possibility that he might stop a bullet himself.

Farther back, in his command-post tent, Colonel Stockton puffed his pipe and looked down at his map table as his executive officer and all his staff officers crowded around, mumbling to each other and pointing at the terrain features. In a corner the communications center was ready for action, as two soldiers wearing headphones sat before two radios, and a third soldier sat at the telephone switchboard. The artillery barrage rumbled in the distance, and every man in the tent glanced at his watch periodically and waited for it to end. The officers in the tent weren't worried about being killed, because their asses weren't on the line; however, they were concerned about their careers and reputations, because if General Hester could be fired, so could they, and it would mean the end of all the ambitions and dreams on which their lives were based. So in a sense they had as much at stake as the men in the foxholes.

A thousand miles away, on the Eighth floor of the AMP Building in Brisbane, Australia, General Douglas MacArthur sat at his desk, looking at communiqués and plans for upcoming operations. The attack on Munda Point on the island of New Georgia was only one small particle of information among the vast concerns in his mind, because he held the responsibility for the conduct of the entire land war in the Pacific.

Battles were raging throughout his combat zone from Malaya to New Guinea, and on numerous little islands that no one had ever heard of before. He had to orchestrate everything so that they would contribute most effectively to his overall goal, the defeat of Japan; but he had another more personal goal that dogged him every moment of the day, and that was his return to the Philippines. He had said that he would return and he had to keep his word, although the military commanders in Washington thought the Philippines should be bypassed in favor of a bold stroke aimed directly at the Japanese home islands.

MacArthur had to fight the Japs and the Joint Chiefs of Staff in Washington. He had to fight his own weaknesses and tendencies toward grandiosity. And on top of everything else, his name was being bandied about as a possible candidate for president of the United States on the Republican ticket in the 1944 elections.

He had a lot on his mind, but he had a vast staff to help him and he was a brilliant man. Many believed he was the greatest military commander in the United States Army, greater than Patton, Bradley, and even Ike, who had once been one of MacArthur's assistants, a fact that galled MacArthur, since Ike now was above him in authority.

In his office, which was decorated with photographs of his wife, young son, politicians, and military men, General MacArthur masterminded the ground war in the South Pacific, trying to hold everything together and move it forward in a systematic way. If his troops lost in one sector and won in four others, he would consider it a good day.

But on New Georgia, there was only one battle facing the

Twenty-third regiment, and they had to win it. Colonel Stockton looked at his watch; and 0700 hours was approaching, the time his regiment was supposed to jump off. Like the men in the field, he wore a steel pot and carried a loaded weapon, his Colt .45 service pistol, which lay cold inside the regulation holster attached to his cartridge belt.

"Take over here, Bates," he said to Lieutenant Colonel Donald Bates, his executive officer. "Private Levinson and Lieutenant Harper, come with me."

Everyone watched as Colonel Stockton left the tent, followed by Lieutenant Harper, one of his aides, and Private Levinson, who carried the backpack radio that would keep Stockton in touch with his headquarters and units. The staff officers didn't approve of what Colonel Stockton was going to do, but they had to accept it. He was going to lead the attack personally to show his men that he was their leader in deed as well as on the books. Colonel Stockton knew that news spread fast on the grapevine, and within an hour or two the entire regiment would know that he was leading them into battle, facing the same dangers as they, while by that time he would be back in his command-post tent, moving pieces of wood around the map table, if he didn't get shot first.

He trudged toward the front line, the lanyard at the bottom of his holster flapping back and forth and his steel pot low over his eyes. His rear echelon soldiers saw him go and watched with awe until the jungle swallowed him up, and then he came to the front lines, in clear view of the Japs on the other side of no-man's land; but he didn't falter or hold his head low, because Colonel Stockton believed that a commanding officer had to be braver than his men if he wanted them to believe in him, and in fact he *was* brave, for he had the mystical notion that he led a charmed life and that no Jap could kill him.

Usually he went to war with his recon platoon, but he was angry at them now, so he made his way to B Company and found the foxhole where its commander, Captain Leonard Goldroy from Topeka, Kansas, huddled with his runner and first sergeant.

"Good morning!" said Colonel Stockton in his booming voice, cheerful and confident, a big smile on his face as if he were on a hunting trip. "No, don't bother getting up—it's okay—as you were!"

They saluted and murmured greetings, more nervous than

ever now that the colonel was hovering over them.

"Well," said Colonel Stockton, "the barrage will stop in about five minutes. I trust you're all set to move out."

"Yes, sir," replied Captain Goldroy, a beefy man with a round face and Band-Aid on his nose where he'd been clipped by a branch during the night march to the company's present position.

"Good," said Colonel Stockton. "Just follow me and everything will be just fine."

"Yes, sir."

Crack! A bullet flew over Colonel Stockton's head, and he looked toward the Japanese lines.

"Sons of bitches couldn't hit a barn door with a wet towel," he said, getting salty, because he knew the men at the front liked him that way.

"I think you'd better get down, sir," Captain Goldroy said.

"What for? The slant-eyed bastards can't hit anything because they see everything on a slant."

Crack!

"See what I mean?" Colonel Stockton asked, casually raising his binoculars to his eyes.

Bullets continued to whistle around Colonel Stockton, but he felt no fear. He'd conquered his physical fear long before, when he'd been a young officer in the First World War. The only fear he hadn't been able to overcome was his fear of failure. That he couldn't countenance. He couldn't permit anything like that to happen to him.

All the soldiers nearby stared at him, expecting him to get shot at any moment. They wondered how he could stand up like that in the face of the sporadic enemy fire; he seemed to be almost superhuman in their eyes, impervious to death, above them in rank but also in courage and everything else. He was like a god to them instead of a colonel.

This of course was the effect Colonel Stockton was trying to achieve. Men followed an officer into battle because of the insignia on his collar, but they put out that extra amount of effort that won battles when they were inspired by his guts and brains and by the example he set.

Besides, he knew the Japs couldn't see him that distinctly in the jungle with bombs falling all around them. He wasn't *that* courageous.

At 0700 hours the barrage stopped, and Colonel Stockton

stepped out resolutely into no-man's-land. He pulled his Colt .45, checked the clip, rammed a round into the chamber, and walked toward the tree line in front of him. All the GIs in the vicinity could see him, and they knew the attack was about to begin. Their mouths went dry and they gripped their weapons tightly. Not far away, the recon platoon could see him, and they felt remorseful, because usually when he went into battle he went with them.

Colonel Stockton raised his pistol hand high in the air, aiming the barrel at the sky. *"Up and at 'em!"* he hollered. *"Follow me!"*

He ran toward the jungle all by himself, and the men behind him came up out of their foxholes to follow him, while up and down the Twenty-third Regiment's line the order was passed along that the attack was under way. The men swept forward and entered the jungle, carrying their rifles at port arms, searching through the branches and leaves for Japs, ready to kill or be killed.

Meanwhile, in the jungle, the Japs crawled out of their hiding places and raised their rifles to their shoulders. They opened fire sporadically at first, and then the shots increased in number until they became a long continuous fusillade.

Colonel Stockton couldn't see much except the trembling of leaves in front of him and clouds of Japanese gunsmoke, but he continued to advance, firing his Colt .45, still setting the example. Lieutenant Harper and Pfc. Levinson followed him, expecting him to get shot down at any moment. Bullets whizzed all around them, and then in the distance they heard the thump-thump-thump of mortar rounds being fired.

The only thing to do in a mortar barrage is run through it, because if you stayed in one spot you'd be blown to bits. Colonel Stockton pumped his pistol hand up and down in the air, the signal to double-time.

"Forward!" he yelled. *"Double-time! Move it out!"*

Colonel Stockton ran forward into the jungle as the mortar rounds rained down on the Twenty-third Regiment. His men followed, drawing their heads into their collars like turtles, feeling bits of trees and clods of mud striking their uniforms. Some were in the wrong place at the wrong time and were blown into the air, arms and legs separated from torsos, heads blasted into tiny pieces.

The Twenty-third ran like wild devils through the jungle, trying to get away from the mortar barrage. Colonel Stockton still was in front of them, urging them on, firing his Colt .45. The mortar barrage crept forward but couldn't keep up with him, and soon they were through it, drawing closer to the first Japanese line of defense.

It consisted of a series of trench fortifications intended to stop or at least slow down any advance, and the Japs inside the trench opened fire on the Americans charging toward them. They had machine guns spaced evenly across their line with overlapping fields of fire, and they sent out a hail of bullets toward the advancing GIs.

It was so intense that the attack faltered. Even Colonel Stockton, with all his courage and determination, dropped down to his stomach and tried to get a picture of what was ahead. He raised his binoculars to his eyes but couldn't see much. He knew his men would be cut to shreds if they tried any wild cavalry charges. The only thing to do was advance unit by unit, utilizing the principles of fire and maneuver, one bunch of GIs covering another bunch that tried to close with the Japanese line. Bullets whistled over his head and he motioned for Pfc. Levinson to move forward and bring him the radio so that he could issue the appropriate orders.

Meanwhile, a few hundred yards away, the recon platoon was pinned down. Lieutenent Breckenridge peered around the trunk of a tree and tried to figure out which squad to send forward first. Somehow they'd have to get close enough so they could jump into those trenches and go to work with their bayonets.

"Where's my machine guns?" he yelled. "Where's my mortars?"

In the First Squad, Butsko lay underneath a bush and hoped a stray Japanese bullet didn't hit the fuel tank on his back, otherwise he'd be roasted alive. Next to him Bannon chewed the soggy butt of a cigarette.

"If I was Colonel Stockton," Butsko said, "I'd pull back the regiment and let the artillery take care of that line."

"I don't think he's gonna pull back after we've come this far."

"Yeah, the old fuck don't like to give up ground once he's got it."

They heard the voice of Lieutenant Breckenridge coming at them through the jungle. *"First Squad—forward! Squads Two and Three—cover them!"*

"Uh-oh," said Butsko.

Bannon swallowed hard and looked down at his M 1 rifle. "I'm so sick of this war," he said, his guts quaking.

Butsko didn't say anything. He just gritted his teeth and wished he was somewhere else. *I'm gonna die today,* he thought. *I just know it.*

"You heard him!" yelled Pfc. Longtree. *"Let's go!"*

The First Squad moved forward, just as squads all across the Twenty-third Regiment's line moved forward, covered by other squads and heavy-weapons platoons. Butsko let the others go first because he was the man with the flamethrower and he was supposed to lag behind and be ready in case his particular talents were needed.

Bannon crawled over the jungle, his M 1 rifle cradled in his arms, hearing bullets being fired all around him. The racket was so fierce that it was difficult to know who was firing what, and bullets zipped over his head or slammed into the ground near him. Gradually the American fire forced the Japanese soldiers to take cover more often and fire less accurately. Inch by inch the First Squad moved closer to the Japanese trenches.

"Second Squad—move out!" yelled Lieutenant Breckenridge. *"Squads One and Three—cover them!"*

Bannon raised his rifle to his shoulder and fired toward the trench system in front of him. It was well camouflaged but he could see the puffs of smoke that gave the Japs away. He aimed carefully and squeezed his rounds as the Second Squad advanced. The metal clip flew into the air after he fired the last bullet, and he reached into a bandolier, taking out a fresh clip and stuffing it in.

"Squad Three—move forward!"

The recon platoon moved forward squad by squad, covering each other, diminishing the distance between them and the Japanese trenches. Private Dunlop in the Third Squad was shot between the eyes, and Corporal Stark in the Second Squad stopped a bullet with his rib cage. The recon platoon had a new medic named Gundy, a conscientious objector who would not shoot at anybody but who consented to help the wounded. He was a pale young man with a sensitive face, blond hair, and wire rimmed spectacles taped to his face so they wouldn't fall off. He crawled through the hellfire and pulled Corporal Stark behind a tree, where he could examine his wound without getting shot himself.

The recon platoon was only twenty yards from the Japanese trenches now, and the Japanese soldiers inside weren't firing as much as they had before because the GIs were devastating them with firepower. Lieutenant Breckenridge thought he was close enough to rush the Japanese line and bust through, but if he stayed where he was, he'd slowly lose more men in a battle of attrition.

"Nutsy!" he yelled. "Gimme my walkie-talkie!"

Nutsy Gafooley was right beside him, and he handed the walkie-talkie over. Lieutenant Breckenridge called Captain Ilecki, the commanding officer of Able Company, to whom the recon platoon was temporarily attached.

"Sir," he said, "request permission to assault!"

"Where are you?" asked Ilecki, taken by surprise.

"Close enough to assault."

"Hmmm," said Captain Ilecki, trying to make a quick decision in the tumult of battle. "I think you'd better wait for the rest of us to catch up."

"We're too close to wait. We either have to attack or pull back, because it's hot here."

"Then maybe you'd better pull back."

"I think it'd be less costly to advance, and if you follow us in, we can crack the line."

"Follow you in?" asked Captain Ilecki, horrified.

"Yes, follow us in. We'll jump off in about two minutes. Over and out."

"Wait a minute!" shouted Captain Ilecki.

But the connection was already broken. Lieutenant Breckenridge handed the walkie-talkie back to Nutsy Galfooley. *"Sergeant Cameron!"*

"Yo!"

"Get over here!"

Sergeant Cameron was twenty feet away. He crawled underneath the fire and madness toward Lieutenant Breckenridge, keeping his head so low that his chin dragged over the leaves and grass.

"Sir?" he said upon arriving.

"We're going to assault the trench. Put out a BAR man on our left flank to protect us there, and put another one on our right flank. We jump off in"—he looked at his watch—"exactly three minutes, so move out!"

"Yes, sir!"

Lieutenant Breckenridge pulled out his canteen and took a sip of water because he had cotton mouth. He tapped a fresh clip of ammo into his carbine and placed the half-filled clip into the pocket of a bandolier. He looked at his watch and had a minute and a half to go. Somebody screamed to his left; another of his men was hit. Somebody called for the medic and Gundy crawled in the direction of the wounded man. The GIs in the recon platoon shot at the Japs, who shot back at them. The battle was at a stalemate, but it wouldn't stay that way for very long.

"Sir!" shouted Nutsy Gafooley. "Captain Ilecki wants to talk with you!"

"Tell him I'm not around! Tell him my attack is under way and I'm expecting him to support me!"

"Yes, sir!"

Lieutenant Breckenridge looked at his watch; the little second hand ticked around the face. His skin tingled and his teeth buzzed with excitement. He intended to lead the men forward just as Colonel Stockton led the regiment, and he knew that he might not make it, but he'd made it all the other times and he hoped he would this time too. Anyway, it wasn't a good idea to worry about things like that. Let the Japs worry.

The second hand on his watch touched the twelve, and he jumped up.

"Take that trench!" he hollered. *"Follow me!"*

He ran toward the trench. The air around him was filled with bullets. He remembered that he'd forgotten to click his carbine into its automatic mode, so he did that as he ran.

"Get 'em!" he yelled. *"Blood and guts!"*

"Blood and guts!" replied his men as they leaped to their feet and followed him through the jungle.

They dodged around trees and jumped over fallen logs as they closed in on the Japanese trench network in front of them, firing their rifles from the waist, trying to make the Japs keep their heads down.

"Go!" screamed Lieutenant Breckenridge.

"Yowee!" replied Frankie La Barbara, moving toward the left flank with his BAR.

Bannon let out a rebel yell and Longtree gave an old Apache war whoop. Everybody joined in with his own special battle cry as the recon platoon surged through the jungle. Private Donahue from the Third Squad got shot in the stomach, and Private Berryman from the Second Squad caught one in the throat, but the recon platoon had the Japanese trench right in front of them now. They were almost home.

Lieutenant Breckenridge saw Japanese faces, helmets, and gun barrels straight ahead. An American soldier bellowed in pain a few feet away from him and went crashing to the ground. Lieutenant Breckenridge aimed his carbine into the trench and pulled the trigger. It shook violently in his hands as the hot lead spat out, and Lieutenant Breckenridge leaped into the air, landing on top of a Japanese soldier in the trench.

The Japanese soldier fell to the side under Lieutenant Breckenridge's considerable weight, and Lieutenant Breckenridge toppled onto his ass. All the Japs in the vicinity dived at him with murder in their eyes, and he rolled over, pulling the trigger of his carbine, spraying them with bullets as they fell on him.

They landed on top of him, dead or wounded, and he pushed them away with his hefty arms, still firing the carbine, working his way to a kneeling position. Meanwhile the trench filled with GIs, who screamed and shouted wildly, attacking the nearest Japs.

Bannon jumped into the trench and kicked with both his feet, connecting with a Jap's head, nearly taking it off. The Jap went flying backward and Bannon touched down, turned around, and saw a Japanese rifle and bayonet streaking toward his heart. He dodged to the side and the bayonet ripped across his left bicep, drawing blood but doing no real damage.

The sudden pain enraged Bannon, who swung his rifle butt around, connecting with the side of the Jap's face, busting cheekbones and shattering the Jap's eardrum. The Jap fell back unconscious and Bannon was going to run him through, when he saw two Japs coming at him through the trench.

The trench was narrow and the Japs stood shoulder to shoulder as both of them simultaneously lunged toward Bannon with their rifles and bayonets. Bannon backpedaled to get out of the way, and tripped over the Jap he'd kicked in the face. He fell onto his back; the two Japs kept coming, angling their bayonets down at him.

It's all over, Bannon thought without any trace of fear, for he was too hyped up by the action to be afraid, when suddenly out of nowhere came Pfc. Sam Longtree, swinging his rifle like a baseball bat. He came up behind the Japs, swung down, and cracked one of them on the head with such force that blood squirted out of the Jap's nose and ears. The Jap collapsed and Bannon reached up to grab the gleaming bayonet on the rifle held by the other Jap. The sharp bayonet blade sliced into Bannon's hands but he hung on and pushed the bayonet away from him.

The Jap's forward motion impelled the bayonet onward and it buried itself nearly to the hilt in the dirt. Bannon pulled his bleeding hands away at the last moment, and Longtree raised his rifle again and brought it down with all his strength. He clobbered the Jap atop his head, fracturing his skull. The Jap collapsed and Bannon jumped to his feet, grabbing his M 1 rifle with his stinging, burning hands.

He barely had time to raise the rifle, when another Jap ran at him with rifle and bayonet aimed for a deathblow. Bannon parried the thrust, smashed the Jap in the face with his rifle butt, and slashed him from his throat to his chest and across to his armpit before he fell down.

Another Jap appeared in front of Bannon, but he was more cautious. He advanced stealthily with his long Arisaka rifle and bayonet, and when he came close he feinted, hoping to make Bannon reach and open up. Bannon lunged forward and plunged his bayonet into the Jap's heart. The Jap looked stunned, because he couldn't believe he had been outmaneuvered so quickly in the game. He sagged to his knees and Bannon pulled back on his rifle, but it was stuck in the Jap's ribs and he couldn't pull it loose. He tugged again; still it wouldn't come out.

He heard the pounding of footsteps behind him and turned around to see a Japanese officer pointing a Nambu pistol directly at him as he charged. Bannon dived at the officer's ankles as the Nambu fired. The bullet cracked over Bannon's head, burying into the ass of a Japanese soldier behind him who was fighting it out with Corporal Gomez from the Second Squad.

Bannon's full weight hit the Japanese officer at the level of his shins, and the Japanese officer fell backward, trying to take aim at Bannon without shooting off his own leg. Bannon grabbed the officer's pistol arm and kneed him in the balls, but the officer twisted to the side and Bannon's knee landed against the officer's hip.

The officer reached up and grabbed for Bannon's head, trying to stick his thumb into Bannon's eye, and Bannon drew back his right hand while holding the officer's pistol hand with his own left hand. He punched down with all his strength and flattened the officer's nose. The officer tried to pull himself together, but he didn't know where he was, and his grip loosened on the Nambu pistol. Bannon plucked it out of his hand, held it by the barrel, and hammered down. The handle of the pistol whacked the officer's forehead and made a dent in the bone. The officer would never wake up again.

Bannon turned the pistol around in his hands so he could hold it to fire, but he had difficulty because there was something wrong with his grip. Some of the tendons in his hands were cut and blood still was flowing. He held the pistol with both hands and got to his feet. In front of him, about ten feet away, a Jap who had his back to him was fighting with Nutsy Gafooley. Butsko stumbled toward the Jap, aimed with both hands, and pulled the trigger. A red hole appeared on the back of the Jap's shirt and he pitched forward onto Nutsy, who fell onto his ass.

Bannon heard running footsteps and spun around. A Jap with fixed bayonet charged him and Bannon shot him between the eyes, then stepped to the side to let the Jap pass by and fall onto his face.

The trench was full of GIs and Japs grunting and cursing, trying to kill each other at close range. Their feet came down on the bodies of GIs and Japs who had been killed or wounded in the fight. On the left flank Frankie La Barbara stood with his BAR, machine-gunning Japs trying to attack from that direction. In front of him were piles of dead Japs, and whenever a head appeared over the top of the pile, Frankie shot it off. The trench was so narrow and filled with the Japs Frankie had killed that no new Japs could get through without being gunned down by him.

The bolt of his BAR slammed home and nothing happened, which indicated that he was out of ammo. He pressed the button that ejected the clip, rammed in a fresh one, and resumed his fire. The BAR pumped bullets out at the Japs trying to fire around the heaps of dead bodies. So far he was able to hold off the Japs on the left flank of the attack.

On the right flank Pfc. Sears, the BAR man from the Third Squad, held his finger against the trigger and raked Japs coming at him from that direction, but one of the Japs lying in the trench got off a lucky shot that hit Sears in the shoulder, spinning him around and knocking him down, opening the right flank to attack.

And attack the Japs did. They saw the way was clear and charged down the trench, hoping to surprise the GIs, who were so busy fighting they didn't see the threat.

But Butsko saw it. He was lying behind the trench, because he couldn't fight hand-to-hand with the flamethrower apparatus on his back. He jumped up and ran toward the part of the trench that Sears had guarded, holding the nozzle of the flamethrower in both his hands. The Japs jumped over the bodies of their fallen comrades and didn't notice him, so intent were they on getting to the GIs in the center of the trench.

Butsko jumped in their path, landing in the bottom of the trench, and as his feet touched down he pressed the trigger. With a loud *shoooooosssshhh* the flaming jellied gasoline shot out of the nozzle and enveloped the Japs in hell. They screeched horribly as they roasted and fried, writhing like snakes and trying to run away, but there was no refuge from the fire that consumed them. They fell to the ground and the odor of burning meat filled the trench. The wind blew it into the part of the trench where the fighting was taking place.

Butsko turned off the trigger to conserve fuel, and mounds of Japs lay in front of him, the jellied gasoline still burning up their bodies, blackened and sputtering like bacon in a frying pan. The odor was ghastly, and Butsko pinched his nose so he wouldn't smell it as he peered down the trench, trying to see if any more Japs were coming.

Meanwhile, in the center of the trench, Lieutenant Breckenridge was spinning around like a whirling dervish, holding his carbine by the barrel and clobbering Japs. They lay all around him with fractured skulls; he'd hit some of them so solidly that their heads had cracked open and their brains were splattered everywhere.

180

He was jubilant, because he knew his men were beating the Japs in that section of the trench. Only a few scattered Japs were still alive and fighting, but he knew that more Japs would attack his flanks before long and he wondered where Able Company was. He turned around to look but couldn't see them coming. How long could the recon platoon hold out in that section of the trench without help?

"*Japs!*" shouted Nutsy Gafooley.

Lieutenant Breckenridge raised his head and saw two platoons of Japs erupt from the jungle straight ahead and charge the trench. They were reinforcements sent in from the Japanese rear, and if they ever got into the trench, they'd out numbered the GIs.

"*Stop them!*" Lieutenant Breckenridge hollared. "*Open fire!*"

The exhausted GIs, splattered with blood and gore, fell against the rear wall of the trench, and opened fire at the charging Japs. Their rifles and BARS barked and rattled, filling the air with smoke and deafening noise, cutting down the Japs who stumbled and fell or pirouetted eerily, dropping their rifles as their blood spurted in spirals in the air.

But there were a lot of them and they kept charging into the barrage. Butsko steadied himself against the wall of the trench and pressed the nozzle of his flamethrower. The fiery gasoline leaped out of the nozzle and splashed over the front row of Japanese soldiers, stopping them in their tracks and covering them with a raging inferno. They shrieked and fell to their knees as the jellied gasoline burned into their flesh and melted their bones.

The attack faltered, but the flanks of the GIs were wide open and more Japs attacked from the sides. The GIs had to divert their fire to protect their flanks, and then more Japs charged out of the jungle to the west. Lieutenant Breckenridge saw that the Japs were determined to recapture that section of the line, and began to doubt that he and his men could hold it. *Where the hell is Able Company?* he thought. He looked behind him but couldn't see any GIs coming to his aid out of the jungle. He was excited and nervous and thought that maybe he should retreat while most of the recon platoon still was intact.

"Gimme the walkie-talkie!" he yelled at Nutsy Gafooley.

Nutsy handed it over, and Lieutenant Breckenridge called

Able Company, but there was no answer. He decided to call battalion headquarters, but Butsko suddenly appeared beside him, holding the smoke nozzle of his flamethrower.

"Sir, we'd better get out of here!" Butsko said.

"I was just calling Battalion for help!"

"We don't have the time!"

Lieutenant Breckenridge glanced around and could see that the recon platoon was in trouble, being attacked on three sides. If the Japs decided to work around behind them, they'd be surrounded.

"Let's get out of here!" Lieutenant Breckenridge yelled. *"Retreat!"*

That was the command the GIs were hoping for, and they climbed out of the trench, heading back toward the safety of the American lines. The Japs behind them saw them going and opened fire at their backs. Private Sanchez from the Fourth Platoon got shot squarely in the back, and Nutsy Gafooley stopped a bullet with the right cheek of his ass.

Nutsy felt as if he'd been kicked by a mule, and was knocked onto his stomach. In all his months of hard fighting on Guadalcanal, this was the first time he'd ever been shot. He was surprised as much as he was in pain, but that lasted only for a few seconds, and then he went into shock.

Lieutenant Breckenridge was behind him when he fell, and he picked Nutsy up by the scruff of the neck, carrying him along to safety. Corporal Tanner from the Second Squad was shot in the left shoulder and he, too, collapsed onto the ground. Tommy Shaw was behind him and heaved him up onto his shoulder, not missing a step as he ran for shelter.

Dragging Nutsy Gafooley along, Lieutenant Breckenridge tasted bitter defeat on his tongue. He now thought that he never should have attacked that trench without support, and that his men were being cut down because of him. He'd made the wrong decision. It had been a crazy, irresponsible thing to do.

Then, before his disbelieving eyes, he saw hordes of GIs debouching from the jungle ahead of him. At first he thought he might be hallucinating, but then he heard his men cheering and knew it was no hallucination. It must be Able Company moving up to help out! The situation wasn't as bad as he'd thought!

"Back to the trench!" he shouted to his men. *"Take that trench!"*

The recon platoon turned around and led the mad charge to the trench. The Japanese soldiers were still getting reorganized and weren't prepared for an attack of such magnitude. Lieutenant Breckenridge dropped the unconscious Nutsy Gafooley onto the ground and fired his carbine ahead of him like a submachine gun as he galloped toward the trench. The Japs in the trench stumbled over dead and wounded bodies as they tried to fight off the Americans, but the recon platoon and Able Company thundered forward and dived into the trench.

The vicious hand-to-hand combat began again, but this time the GIs greatly outnumbered the Japanese and overwhelmed them totally. There were five minutes of stabbing and shooting at close quarters, and then all the Japs were dead or wounded. The GIs had cracked the Japanese line.

Captain Ilecki and Lieutenant Breckenridge positioned their men in the trench for the major Japanese counterattack that they expected any moment, because the Japanese always liked to counterattack quickly while the Americans were tired and low on ammunition. Captain Ilecki and Lieutenant Breckenridge ordered machine-gun crews on the flanks to protect them from those directions, but their main effort was directed toward the jungle ahead, where the Japs kept their reserves.

It didn't take long to put the men in place, and then Lieutenant Breckenridge joined Captain Ilecki in the center of the trench.

"You'd better call Battalion for help," Lieutenant Breckenridge said. "If the Japs attack in force, we might not be able to hold them off."

"Already called them," said Captain Ilecki, a lanky man with delicate features marred by an old combat scar on his left cheek.

"Here they come!" yelled somebody from Able Company.

Japs poured out of the jungle straight ahead, screaming *"Banzai!"* and shaking their rifles and bayonets. Their bared their teeth like wild animals as they raced toward the trench, and the GIs opened fire in a massive fusillade, ripping apart their first wave, but the second and third waves charged past their fallen comrades.

American bullets whistled around them, but the Japs never

hesitated or faltered in their charge. Leading them was an officer swinging a samurai sword, a red sash wrapped around his waist. He made a wonderful target, and about twenty bullets hit him almost simultaneously. Vomiting blood, he dropped to the ground and a sergeant picked up his samurai sword, continuing the charge, but he, too, was shot down; then a Japanese private picked it up, running forward on his short legs and screaming *"Banzai!"*

When the Japs came within flamethrower range, Butsko pressed the trigger on the nozzle, and the flaming jelly spewed out, gobs of it landing on the Japanese soldiers, who were surprised, then horrified, then cooked alive. Butsko swung the nozzle from side to side, splashing the Japs with flame, and then aimed high so it would drop down on them like rain.

The leading ranks of Japanese soldiers were shot down by the GIs, and Butsko burned up a substantial number, but the rest continued their wild banzai charge and swarmed into the trench. Bayonets glinted in the sun and shots rang out at close quarters. Men stabbed and gouged each other, grunting and snarling, locked in mortal combat.

Butsko threw off his flamethrower gear because he couldn't fight with it, and pulled his Ka-bar knife out of its scabbard, because it was the only weapon he had for hand-to-hand fighting. Before the tip of the blade got clear of the scabbard, a Jap with a samurai sword landed in front of him, raised the sword in the air, and swung down at Butsko's head.

Butsko darted to the side and the blade clanged against the dirt and rocks piled up on the rim of the trench. Butsko slashed sideways with his knife and cut across the Jap's stomach, twisting the blade around on the backswing and severing the Jap's windpipe. The Jap fell to the ground and Butsko plucked the samurai sword out of his hand, returned his Ka-Bar to its scabbard, saw a Jap fighting a GI in front of him, and swung the samurai sword sideways into the Jap's kidney.

The Jap screamed hysterically and looked at the sky, reaching around to hold his kidney together, and the GI in front of him ran him through with the bayonet on the end of his rifle. The Jap fell onto his back and Butsko stepped on his face as he charged down the trench, holding the samurai sword high in the air.

He swung down with all his strength and split the skull of

a Japanese soldier in two like a coconut. Pulling the sword from the Jap's collarbone, he swung diagonally, catching a Jap at the juncture of his neck and shoulders. cracking downward through six of the Jap's ribs.

The sword got stuck in the bones and gristle. Butsko pulled with all his strength but couldn't loosen it. A Jap screamed a few feet away from him, thrusting his rifle and bayonet forward, and Butsko grabbed the barrel of the rifle with both hands, stopping its forward motion. The Jap was surprised by this sudden feat of incredible power, and tried to pull the rifle away from Butsko, but Butsko held it in his viselike grip and pulled with all his strength, angling his head downward. The Jap wouldn't let go of his rifle but didn't have the strength to hold his ground. His face crashed into Butsko's helmet, bashing his nose into a pancake. Stunned, the Jap's legs wobbled and he loosened his grip. Butsko yanked the rifle out of the Jap's hands and bashed him in the face with the rifle butt. The Jap collapsed onto his back and again Butsko slammed him in the face with the rifle butt, busting the Jap's head apart, brains splattering in all directions.

A bit of the Jap's brain flew onto Butsko's lip, and he spat it away, turning to face a Japanese soldier advancing with rifle and bayonet. *"Banzai!"* the Jap hollered, lunging at Butsko, the Jap's bayonet stained with American blood.

Butsko put all of his weight into a parry, pushing the Jap's rifle and bayonet to the side. The forward motion of both soldiers caused their shoulders to collide, and Butsko's face came to within three inches of the Jap's. They looked into each other eyes, saw the fury and bloodlust, and pulled back to try to murder each other again.

Butsko feinted with his rifle and bayonet, but the Jap didn't fall for it. He feinted again, and at the same moment the Jap thrust his rifle and bayonet toward Butsko's heart. All Butsko could do was raise his rifle and try to parry the blow, but he didn't have the strength behind the move, and he only deflected the Jap's bayonet up toward his face.

Butsko tried to move out of the way, but he didn't have a chance. The Japanese bayonet dug into his cheek and its tip scraped across his cheekbone to the corner of his ear. The pain was excruciating and Butsko saw red as he instinctively yanked his head to the side, disengaging with the Japanese bayonet before it took off the top of his ear.

The Jap was still in the motion of his forward thrust, off balance, and seeing with horror that he hadn't hurt Butsko much. He was wide open and Butsko punched upward with the butt of his rifle, catching the Jap on the tip of his chin. The blow knocked the Jap's head backward, and Butsko swung sideways, whacking the Jap on the side of the face.

The Jap was dazed, and Butsko turned his rifle around, aimed the bayonet at the Jap's stomach, and pushed it in to the hilt. He withdrew it quickly, and blood poured out of the Jap's stomach. The Jap sagged to the ground at Butsko's feet. Butsko kicked him in the face and looked around for another Jap to kill, but he couldn't find any. The other Japs in his vicinity were either dead or engaged in hand-to-hand combat with GIs. A lot of GIs stood around like Butsko with no Japs to fight. The Japanese counterattack had been stopped cold by the recon platoon and Able Company.

Captain Ilecki and Lieutenant Breckenridge were already planning ahead, getting ready for the next Jap counterattack. As the last Japs in the trench were polished off they shouted orders for the placement of machine-gun crews and mortar squads. They told the rifle soldiers to line up and load up and watch the jungle for more Japs. Meanwhile Pfc. Gundy and the medics from Able Company worked on the wounded GIs. Gundy walked up to Butsko and saw that the side of his face was a mass of blood.

"Lemme look," Gundy said, scrutinizing Butsko's cheek, trying to see where all the blood was coming from.

"It's nothing," Butsko told him, pushing him away. "Take care of somebody else."

Gundy saw a soldier from Able Company coughing blood, his back supported by the wall of the trench. He had a big bubbling wound in his chest and it looked to Gundy as if the soldier's lung had been punctured. He knelt down beside the soldier, and Butsko went looking for his flamethrower. He saw Bannon looking down at the palms of his hands and trying to move his fingers.

"What's the matter with you?" Butsko asked.

"My hands are all fucked up."

"Find a rifle and get into position."

Bannon looked around and saw an M 1 rifle lying on the ground next to a dead GI from Able Company. He picked it up, pulled back the bolt, and saw bullets in the clip in the chamber. Dropping to his knees, he leaned his elbows on the wall of the trench and sighted at the trees in the jungle ahead.

Frankie La Barbara dropped down next to him, gouts of blood all over his uniform, but he hadn't been wounded himself except for a few little nicks and cuts. He was breathing like a horse that had just finished running the Kentucky Derby, and he pushed his helmet back on his head. He looked at Bannon and Bannon looked back at him. They wanted to talk but there was nothing to say. Frankie took out his pack of cigarettes and held them out to Bannon, who took one. They lit up and puffed their cigarettes, gazing at the jungle, ready for any Japs who might attack again.

Frankie wiped his mouth with the back of his hand. He was hungry and thirsty. He closed his eyes and saw bloody, gory corpses of soldiers, then opened his eyes and saw the same thing. Frankie felt eerie and schizoid, as if he were floating above himself and looking down at himself and the carnage in the trench. He puffed his cigarette nervously.

"*Here they come!*" shouted Bannon.

Frankie blinked and looked at the jungle in front of him. Sure enough, the Japs were attacking again, screaming and hollering, trying to rush the trench.

"*Open fire!*" yelled Lieutenant Breckenridge.

The machine-gun crews were set up and the mortars were zeroed in. Everyone cut loose with everything he had, tearing into the hordes of attacking Japs. Butsko got on his knees and held the nozzle of his flamethrower, ready to burn them up when they got close. A few feet away, Longtree aimed his rifle at the Japs, squeezed off a round, aimed again, and squeezed off another round. He continued doing this until his clip emptied and clanged into the air; then he stuffed another clip into his M 1 and squeezed off more rounds. Japs fell in front of him, but he didn't know if he'd shot them or if somebody else had. He wore a big bandage around his left thigh where a Jap had stabbed him during the confused hand-to-hand fighting in the trench.

Frankie shifted his BAR from side to side as he mowed

down the attacking Japanese. Mortar rounds landed in the jungle, blowing the Japs up, and the machine guns peppered the Japs with bullets.

The Japanese attack had been mounted quickly and didn't consist of many men. They continued to charge into the mouths of the American weapons until their officers could see that it was slaughter, ordering a retreat back to the jungle. The Japs turned tail and ran away as the GIs shot them in their backs. The fire was withering and the jungle was carpeted with dead Japs after the live ones disappeared from sight.

Meanwhile, in response to Captain Ilecki's plea for help, Companies B and C hit the trenches on both sides of Company A, and fierce fighting could be heard on all sides. While this was taking place, the battalion commander radioed Colonel Stockton, telling him that the entire trench network could be taken if the rest of the regiment was thrown into the battle.

Colonel Stockton ordered the regiment forward, and by midday the trench network belonged to the Twenty-third Regiment. Colonel Stockton called General Hawkins and asked for permission to press his attack.

"No," General Hawkins said. "Stay right where you are until the rest of the division catches up."

"But I've got the Japs off balance in this sector, sir. If I push hard, I can clear out this whole damned jungle."

"I said stay where you are. I don't want any units moving ahead unless I can secure their flanks."

"I can secure my own flanks, sir."

"I just gave you an order. Stay where you are and send out patrols to see what's in that jungle."

"Yes, sir."

Colonel Stockton handed the radio headset back to Lieutenant Harper and looked down at his map, spread out on the hood of his jeep. It was parked in a little clearing in the jungle, not far from his main line of advance. Bending over the map, he marked the approximate configuration of the trench system and was pleased to note that his regiment had made a huge gain, farther than any other regiment in the division. *I did it again,* he thought. *How many times do I have to do this before I get my star?*

"Lieutenant Harper," he said. "Find out which unit was the

first to crack that trench network."

"It was the First Battalion, sir."

"Which company?"

Lieutenant Harper got on the radio to find out, and Colonel Stockton looked down at his map, trying to figure out the best way to move against Munda Point. He felt happy, because his regiment had taken more ground in one morning than the 169th Regiment had taken in the past two weeks.

Ahead of the trench network were some hills, according to his map. He knew that the Japs were holed up in those hills, because that's the way they'd fought on Guadalcanal. It had been a grim and bloody job, clearing them out on Guadalcanal, but the GIs had done the job and would do it again on New Georgia.

"Sir," said Lieutenant Harper. "I've got the information for you."

Colonel Stockton placed his finger on the hill system depicted on the map and looked up at Lieutenant Harper. "Well?"

Lieutenant Harper was ill at ease. "It was the recon platoon, sir."

Colonel Stockton dropped his pencil. "What!"

"It was the recon platoon, sir. Captain Ilecki reports that the recon platoon invaded the trench first, and Able Company followed them in. Then the rest of the First Battalion exploited the opening."

Colonel Stockton looked as if he'd been hit over the head with a brick. His face went pale and his eyes took on a faraway look. He picked up his pencil and walked away from the map, his brow furrowed.

The recon platoon did it again, he thought. He didn't know whether to be happy or angry. They were a bunch of trouble-makers and madmen, but they always came through for him when he needed them.

He sat on a log and took out his pipe, filling the bowl with the Briggs smoking mixture that he kept in a zippered old pigskin pouch. *The recon platoon cracked the Jap line,* he said to himself. *They're always the ones who lead the way.* Colonel Stockton speculated on how many lives the recon platoon had saved with their bold attack. Maybe hundreds, and days of slow grueling advances. Colonel Stockton admitted that the recon platoon had made him look good again. He thought of Butsko, Bannon, and the others, and couldn't help feeling gratitude.

He lit his pipe, stood, and paced back and forth, his hands clasped behind his back. *What a fine bunch of soldiers they are*, he thought. *They're not good for anything else except for killing Japs, but that's the main thing in this war. They ran into the jaws of hell when they attacked that trench system, but they didn't stop. They are great fighters.*

He knew that Butsko had been instrumental in the operation. And Bannon too. They couldn't stay out of trouble in Honolulu, but the same fighting spirit that had landed them in jail had also landed them inside that Japanese trench.

Hell, Colonel Stockton thought, still pacing back and forth, *they're soldiers just like I am, so why have I been treating them like a bunch of civilians? Who cares what troubles they get into in Honolulu? The main thing is that they win battles for me here.*

The more Colonel Stockton thought about it, the more enthusiastic he became about his recon platoon and the guiltier he felt about the way he'd been treating them. They put their lives on the line for the regiment time and time again, and all he did was worry about getting his star. *To hell with that star*, he thought. *I command the finest goddamn regiment in the Army, and I'm doing what I love, so what do I need that star for?*

He spun around. "Major Cobb!"

"Yes, sir!"

"I'm going to the front! Take charge here until I return!"

"Yes, sir! Where will you be if I need you!"

"With Able Company! Where's my driver!"

"Here, sir!"

"We're going to the front! Get that jeep started! Lieutenant Harper, you're coming too!"

"Yes, sir!"

Major Cobb cleared the maps off the hood of the Jeep, and the driver, Private Nick Bombasino from Philadelphia, got behind the wheel, revving it up. Colonel Cobb sat beside him in the front seat, still puffing his pipe, and Lieutenant Harper jumped into the backseat.

"Go!" said Colonel Stockton.

Nick Bombasino shifted into gear, and the wheels of the jeep spun in the muck before catching hold and carrying the jeep away into the jungle. Major Cobb watched them go and took off his helmet wiping the sweat from his forehead with the back of his arm.

"I knew this would happen," he muttered to the staff officers standing nearby. "I knew the recon platoon would get back in his good graces before long."

SIXTEEN . . .

Lieutenant Breckenridge sat inside the trench as Private Gundy bandaged a cut on his scalp. Nearby, the men were eating C rations out of cans, their weapons close by in case the Japs attacked again.

Lieutenant Breckenridge felt exhausted in mind and body. The morning had been packed with action, and now for the first time he was able to let himself feel the fatigue. He hoped some C rations and coffee would perk him up again.

Corporal Gomez appeared, running along the ground on the top of the trench. "Sir!" he said. "Colonel Stockton is here!"

Lieutenant Breckenridge pushed Private Gundy away and stood up. "Where?"

"Over there!" Corporal Gomez pointed toward the American rear.

"Sir," said Private Gundy, "let me finish with the bandage."

"Hurry up."

Private Gundy pressed on the last inch of adhesive, and Lieutenant Breckenridge put on his helmet and slung his carbine. He climbed out of the trench, looked around, and saw Colonel Stockton, followed by Lieutenant Harper, walking toward the trench.

Lieutenant Breckenridge headed toward Colonel Stockton, who noticed him and veered in his direction. Colonel Stockton was smiling and Lieutenant Breckenridge felt relieved, because he thought he might have done something wrong. Lieutenant Breckenridge came to within ten feet of Colonel Stockton, stopped, and saluted. Colonel Stockton stopped and returned the salute.

"At ease," he said.

Lieutenant Breckenridge moved closer to Colonel Stockton, who could see the bottom of the bandage under Lieutenant Breckenridge's helmet.

"What happened to your head?" Colonel Stockton asked. "Nothing serious, I hope?"

"Just a scratch, sir. Nothing to worry about."

Colonel Stockton looked at the trench system. "I understand the recon platoon was the first unit to crack that Jap trench."

"I believe that's so, sir."

Colonel Stockton slapped Lieutenant Breckenridge on the arm. "Congratulations. It was a magnificent feat of arms."

"I didn't do it, sir. It was the men."

"The men are always the ones who do it, but you're their commanding officer and everything they do is a reflection of your leadership."

Lieutenant Breckenridge smiled. "I'm not so sure about that, sir. I think I was just along for the ride."

"We're all just along for the ride, but there wouldn't be any ride at all without us."

"If you say so, sir."

Colonel Stockton hooked his thumbs in his cartridge belt and looked Lieutenant Breckenridge over. "If you keep this up, you'll have your company before you know it."

Lieutenant Breckenridge pinched his lips together and looked thoughtful. "I don't know about that now, sir. I think I might want to stay where I am for a while. I like the recon platoon. They're real soldiers for a change. You don't have to work to make them do what's necessary. They know what to do and they follow through without being told. They're professionals. It's easy to be an officer with men like these."

Lieutenant Stockton puffed his pipe. "It couldn't have been that easy. I saw a lot of Jap casualties between my headquarters and here."

"It would have been a lot harder without the recon platoon. My old platoon in King Company couldn't have done it."

"I want to see the men. Where are they?"

"Down in there," Lieutenant Breckenridge said, pointing toward the trench.

Colonel Stockton strode toward the trench and jumped inside, landing next to Corporal Gomez, whose left bicep was bandaged.

"Ten-*hut!*" yelled Gomez.

"As you were!" replied Colonel Stockton.

Lieutenant Breckendrige dropped into the trench and landed beside Colonel Stockton, who was shaking the bewildered Corporal Gomez's hand.

"Good work, soldier," Colonel Stockton said.

"Thank you, sir," replied Gomez.

Colonel Stockton walked among the men shaking their hands and patting their backs, telling jokes, trying to put them at ease. But he never could put them completely at ease because he lived in a different world than they and everybody knew it.

He could see that they were tired and bloody, wearing bandages, in the state of blissful shock that follows a victorious battle. He looked into their bloodshot eyes and felt love for them, for they were his men, his own soldiers, who followed his orders and won glory for him and themselves.

His eyes misted up and he felt like a traitor for pursuing his general's star, because if he got it he'd have to leave his men, and now, shoulder to shoulder with them in the trench, he wanted to stay with them forever. What could be better than to command a regiment of men like these? If he became a general, he'd be assigned to some other general's staff, and he wouldn't be a combat commander anymore. He'd just be another staff officer, and men like these in the trench would have contempt for him.

He could smell blood mixed with the dirt in the trench, and could sense the violence of the battle that had taken place there only an hour before. He saw Frankie La Barbara, his uniform splattered with Jap blood, sitting on his haunches, eating a can of C rations.

Colonel Stockton kneeled beside him. "Hello, Frankie," he said. "How're you doing?"

"Just fine, sir."

"Keep up the good work."

Colonel Stockton patted his shoulder and continued down the trench. He knew that all eyes were on him and he smiled, nodding to the men, shaking their hands, thanking them for the great job they'd done.

He saw Longtree with a bandage on his thigh. "Good fighting," he said, shaking Longtree's hand.

"Thank you, sir."

Colonel Stockton walked past Longtree and saw more men from the recon platoon with their torn uniforms and haggard faces. *I love these men,* Colonel Stockton thought. *They're the greatest soldiers in the world.*

His eyes fell on Bannon and Butsko, standing side by side, looking at him. Bannon's hands were bandaged and Butsko wore a bandage that covered the left side of his face. Their uniforms were mangled and they'd taken their helmets off so they could get some cool air on their heads.

These men have bled for me, Colonel Stockton thought as he walked toward them. *They've bled for me many times, and I've repaid them by taking away their stripes because they got in a little trouble in Honolulu.*

He walked up to Butsko and held out his hand. Butsko hesitated a moment, then reached out and shook hands with Colonel Stockton.

"I know this attack couldn't have succeeded without you, Butsko," Colonel Stockton said.

"I just did my job, sir," Butsko replied.

"You did it well, Butsko, and I think you should be the platoon sergeant here, just as you used to be."

Everybody nearby was looking at Butsko, and he shuffled his feet self-consciously. "If you say so, sir."

"I say so. You're a master sergeant again."

"Yes, sir."

"Keep up the good work."

"Yes, sir."

Their eyes locked on to each other, and the old warmth and friendship returned. It was based on the mutual respect of two old soldiers who'd been to hell and back, and nothing could interfere with it for long. Colonel Stockton turned and held out his hand to Bannon.

"You're a corporal again, Bannon. You're starting with a fresh slate as of now."

"Thank you, sir."

They shook hands, and Colonel Stockton's fingers wrapped around the bandages on Bannon's hands.

"Hands okay?" Colonel Stockton asked.

"I can still pull a trigger," Bannon replied.

"Good man. Carry on." Colonel Stockton looked meaningfully at Sergeant Butsko. "I'll be talking with you again soon."

"Yes, sir."

Colonel Stockton turned and walked away, shaking more hands, patting more backs, chatting with his men, happy to be with them in the trenches, deeply moved by the gallantry and steadfastness of these ordinary American young men who wore Army uniforms and gave their all for their country.

These are my soldiers, he said to himself, *and I never want to leave them. General MacArthur can take that star and shove it up his ass.*

Look for

HOT LEAD AND COLD STEEL

next novel in the new RAT BASTARDS series from Jove

coming in September!